She Quietly Screams

An Artemis Blythe Mystery Thriller

Georgia Wagner

CONTENTS

PROLOGUE

The Seattle boardwalk shone with an effervescent glow, each twinkling light reflecting off the rippling waters of the bay. The scent of saltwater mingled with that of fresh seafood and funnel cakes, wafting through the air as street performers captivated crowds with their vibrant displays of dance, acrobatics, and song. Painters and sculptors displayed their works along the promenade, transforming the ordinary walkway into a living, breathing gallery. It was a symphony of art and culture, a celebration of life that coursed through every corner of the bustling cityscape.

Nothing hinted at what lay around the corner. No one suspected the horrors on the horizon.

Hand in hand, James and Emma strolled beneath the canopy of lights, their laughter bubbling up like champagne. They had just emerged from an evening at the theater, where they had been swept away by the magic of the stage. Their eyes sparkled with the remnants of the performance, their hearts full of wonder and delight.

"Can you believe how incredible that was?" James asked, his voice brimming with excitement.

Emma grinned, her cheeks flushed from giddiness. "I've never seen anything like it before! The costumes, the music, the way they made you feel like you were right there with them!"

As they continued their leisurely pace, they exchanged playful banter about their favorite moments and characters from the show. Every now and then, they would pause at an artist's stall to admire the intricate pieces on display, adding their own commentary and opinions on the various styles.

At one such stall, Emma picked up a delicate glass figurine of a dancer poised en pointe, her limbs gracefully outstretched. "Look, James, it's me!" she giggled, attempting an exaggerated arabesque with her free hand.

James laughed, catching her around the waist as she wobbled precariously. "My dear wife, your talents are many, but I'm not quite sure ballet is one of them."

"Very funny," she mock-pouted before breaking into laughter once more.

As they continued on their way, the jovial atmosphere of the boardwalk seemed to wrap around them like a warm embrace, a haven from the world outside. And for a while, it was as if nothing could touch them—not the pressures of work or the weight of responsibilities that awaited them at home.

The laughter still laced their breaths as they strolled arm-in-arm, the boardwalk's vibrant energy a fading backdrop. The glow of street lamps cast elongated shadows on the cobblestones while the distant murmur of the remaining crowd hummed like an afterthought.

"Hey," James said, his voice lowered to almost a whisper, "how about we take a shortcut? Will give us some extra time for..." His eyes twinkled. "...some fun. We'll be home in no time."

Emma's eyes widened at the narrow passage that snaked between the buildings, darkness swallowing its depths. She swallowed hard, trying to quell the sudden unease bubbling within her. "I don't know, it looks... creepy."

"Aw, come on. It's just a shortcut!" James teased, a playful nudge accompanying his words. "Besides, I'm here to protect you." He flexed his arm with mock bravado, earning a reluctant giggle from Emma.

"Alright," she agreed, reluctant but unwilling to show her fear. They turned into the alley, her grip tightening around his arm as if he were her lifeline. The intimacy of the moment was not lost on her; it was both comforting and unsettling, and she couldn't help but feel vulnerable.

"James, do you hear that?" she asked, her voice barely audible over the pounding of her heart. A faint rustling echoed through the alley, like footsteps crunching on broken glass.

"Probably just a cat or something," he reassured her. But Emma could sense the tension in his grip. The mysterious sound grew louder, closer, transforming the atmosphere into a suffocating dread that clung to them like ivy.

"Maybe we should turn back," she suggested, unable to contain the tremble in her voice any longer. But James shook his head, his jaw set with determination. He had always been stubborn like this. Especially when he thought something might make him seem weak in front of her.

"Ah, it's not a big deal. Let's keep going," he urged, leading her further into the shadows.

As they ventured deeper into the alley, the mysterious sound seemed to chase after them, a lurking presence that gnawed at their nerves.

The darkness seemed to deepen as if swallowing the alley whole.

Emma paused, staring up at a dark smear against the warehouse building. "L-look..." she stammered, pointing.

She'd gone completely still and stared at the strange outline.

There. That's where the sound of footsteps was coming from.

A figure was swaying back and forth as if they had to use the restroom, nervously prancing from one foot to the other and creating a tinny, echoing sound that reverberated strangely in the acoustics of the alley.

It looked as if the figure were standing on a wooden pallet, riveted with rusted metal slats—the makeshift stage was suspended twenty feet in the air under a window of the warehouse, a small terrace made with used plywood and cheap nails.

The shadowy figure standing on a wooden pallet was barely distinguishable from the murkiness that surrounded them. The air grew thick with tension and an eerie silence, which intensified their confusion and curiosity.

"Hello?" James called out hesitantly, his voice echoing off the walls of the alley. There was no response, only the sound of their own ragged breaths.

"James, I don't like this," Emma whispered, her grip on his arm tightening as her eyes remained fixed on the hazy silhouette. "Who is that?"

"Maybe they're just... lost or something," he countered, but he didn't seem convinced by his own words.

"Hey!" James tried again, raising his voice slightly. "Do you need help?" He glanced at Emma, his brow furrowed in concern. She could see the unease etched on his face mirroring her own feelings.

"J-James, let's forget about the shortcut. Let's just go back the way we came," Emma pleaded, her voice laced with urgency. Her heart raced, pounding against her chest, a caged bird desperate for release.

"Alright, alright. We'll leave," he conceded. They began to step back, keeping their gazes locked on the stationary figure whose only movements were the occasional shifting of weight from one foot to the other.

Just as Emma and James were about to turn the corner, a sudden floodlight flickered on, bathing the alley in an unnatural, harsh brightness. They froze and Emma let out a little squeak of fear at the sudden brightness, blinding and startling all at once.

The light came from the roof of the opposite structure, casting the figure on the wooden pallet in full illumination, their features carved in sharp relief against the grimy brick wall.

It was a young woman, standing alone, stranded on the wooden platform above them. Her fingers fretted at the sleeves of her shirt and she looked as startled as Emma was at the light now bathing her, cringing back and shuddering with a silent sob.

A shiver raced down Emma's spine. What was going on here? Who had turned on the light?

"James, we need to go," she urged, her voice barely audible. She could feel a cold sweat forming on her brow, her heart pounding even harder now. But he didn't seem to hear her, his gaze transfixed on the woman now standing under the stark illumination.

Emma followed his line of sight, her breath catching in her throat when she saw it—a small, red laser dot hovering steadily on the young woman's forehead. Her mind raced, connecting the dots with horrifying clarity.

"J-James," she stammered, "that's—"

"Emma, stay calm," he interrupted, his voice tense but controlled. He reached for her hand, gripping it tightly as if to anchor them both to some semblance of safety. "Don't make any sudden movements."

"Who's doing this?" she whispered, her voice quivering with fear.

As the couple edged cautiously away, the figure moved at last. A soft whimper that caused James and Emma to freeze in their tracks, a sound that was undeniably human, filled with pain and fear.

"Please," the woman whispered, her voice trembling. "Please don't go."

The floodlight cast dark shadows across the young woman's face, accentuating the hollows beneath her eyes and the gaunt curve of her cheekbones. Her gaze darted between James and Emma, wide with a twitching terror that threatened to spill into full panic.

"Who are you?" James asked gently, his grip on Emma's hand unwavering.

"Jess," she murmured, her body language betraying her vulnerability. She clutched her arms tightly around herself as if to shield herself from an unseen threat. "I-I need your help."

"Help with what?" Emma inquired, her compassion momentarily overcoming her fear.

"Please, don't make me say it out loud," Jess pleaded, tears streaming down her pale cheeks. "You have to understand, I didn't want any of this." But Emma felt suddenly as if Jess wasn't even speaking to them.

Her pleading wasn't really directed at them but at some unseen person. Perhaps whoever had turned on the lights?

Suddenly, Jess began to raise her voice, shouting, "I've committed sins. The worst thing I've ever done is hard to say... but..." She trailed off, swallowing, tears streaming down her face. "But everyone ought to know the truth." She stammered, her face red, but this was only partially due to the glowing red laser dot on her forehead.

She whimpered but then summoning inner resolve, she declared, "I... I slept with my sister's boyfriend. I didn't mean for it to happen. I also... when I was younger, I stole money from my mother's purse..."

Emma's breath caught in her throat as the words spilled out of Jess's mouth. She could feel the weight of James's gaze on her, but she couldn't look away from the girl standing before them, her soul laid bare.

Jess said, her voice barely above a whisper now, "I need to confess. I need to make things right before it's too late."

Before either of them could respond, there was a sudden commotion from the rooftop where the floodlight had appeared. They heard shouting and the sound of footsteps pounding across the rooftop.

"Jess, you need to get out of there!" James said urgently, tugging Emma's hand as if urging her to walk with him to Jess's platform. But Emma was frozen to the spot.

Jess didn't move either. She stood rooted in place, her eyes fixed on something above them as if she were seeing some apparition.

She sobbed again, then pulled a knife from her waistband where it had been jutting upward like the gleaming handle of a slot machine.

She lifted it.

Emma's heart leapt in her throat.

Jess dragged the knife across her throat with a faint mewl of pain. For one bare moment, she wobbled in place then her limp body toppled off the makeshift wooden stage.

And Emma screamed.

CHAPTER 1

The tires of the black sedan hummed on the slick pavement as Artemis navigated through the winding roads of Washington State's most affluent neighborhood. The opulence of the area unnerved her, but it was nothing compared to the tension she felt sitting next to her sister, Helen.

"Can you believe that house?" Helen asked in a hushed voice, pointing to an enormous mansion that loomed ahead. "It must have at least twelve bedrooms."

Artemis glanced at the imposing structure, then back to the road, her grip on the steering wheel tightening. It wasn't the house that left her feeling disoriented; it was the fact that Helen was even there, speaking with such ease and serenity. A mere month ago, her sister had been a completely different person—volatile, unpredictable, and dangerous. Yet here she was, a picture of tranquility after a series of hypnosis sessions with their father and several medication adjustments.

"Quite something," Artemis mumbled, trying to mask her disbelief. She couldn't help but recall how they used to drive through these streets as children, Helen, always so eager to point out the most extravagant homes and wonder what lay behind their closed doors. But now, with the transformation Helen had undergone, Artemis wondered what lay behind her sister's eyes.

"Artemis, are you okay?" Helen's voice was soft and sweet. "You seem tense."

"Fine," Artemis lied, forcing a smile. She twisted her fingers along the fabric of the shirt she'd ordered online. "Just focusing on the road."

"Of course." Helen nodded understandingly, turning her attention back to the passing scenery. Her calm demeanor was almost unnerving, considering what she had been through. One couldn't imagine this gentle soul was the same person.

As they continued their drive, Artemis couldn't help but steal glances at her sister. She observed the way Helen's fingers gently tapped against her thigh, perfectly in time with the rhythm of the car's turn signal and natural hum.

Her gaze lingered on Helen's serene expression, her eyes closed as if she were savoring each moment of this newfound peace.

"Remember when we used to make up stories about the people who lived in these houses?" Helen asked suddenly, her eyes opening and meeting Artemis'. "We were quite the imaginative duo."

Artemis nodded, her heart aching at the memory. It felt like a lifetime ago when they'd been close enough to share such fantasies. "Yeah," she agreed softly. "We were."

"Let's do it again," Helen suggested, her smile warm and inviting. "Just for old times' sake?"

"Alright," Artemis acquiesced, attempting to put aside her unease. She focused on a sprawling estate with ivy-covered walls and turrets that reached toward the sky. "That one looks like it could be owned by a reclusive billionaire inventor."

"Or a secret society of international spies," Helen added, her eyes twinkling with excitement.

Despite her reservations, Artemis couldn't help but smile at her sister's enthusiasm. Perhaps things could return to some semblance of normalcy between them after all. But deep inside, the tension remained, gnawing away at her hope and leaving her with an ever-growing sense of unease.

Artemis glanced at the rearview mirror, her eyes drawn to the reflection of her sister's serene face. The contrast between Helen's current calmness and the violent alter ego that haunted her thoughts was almost too much for Artemis to bear. It was a revelation she'd discovered by chance: Helen was the infamous Ghost Killer. Her sister's split personality had been responsible for the deaths of several people as well as countless attempts on others.

"Look at that one," Helen said, pointing to a palatial home set back from the road. White columns flanked the grand entrance and ivy crawled up the stone exterior, lending an air of ancient elegance to the estate. "I bet it has a library with floor-to-ceiling bookshelves."

"Probably," Artemis replied, her voice distant as she struggled to reconcile this tender version of her sister with the cold-blooded killer lurking beneath the surface. She swallowed hard, trying to shove the gruesome images away. "And a hidden passage behind one of the shelves."

"Exactly," Helen agreed, laughing softly. "Maybe even a secret, underground lair."

The two sisters continued their game as they cruised down the tree-lined street, admiring the stately homes that served as monuments to the wealth of the area. Each house seemed more opulent than the last, boasting vast lawns adorned with intricate gardens and sparkling fountains.

"Hey, remember that time we snuck into the Harringtons' garden party?" Helen asked, a mischievous smile playing on her lips. "We stuffed our faces with shrimp cocktail and drank champagne like we owned the place."

"Until we got caught," Artemis reminded her, chuckling at the memory. "Then I mainly remember running."

"Good times," Helen sighed, her eyes distant with nostalgia. "I miss those days."

"Me too," Artemis confessed, her voice barely a whisper. She missed the simpler times, before the darkness had taken root in Helen's mind and twisted her into something unrecognizable.

"Artemis?" Helen asked softly, sensing her sister's unease. "Are you sure you're alright?"

"Of course," she lied, forcing a smile. "Just lost in thought."

"About what?" Helen pressed gently, her gaze filled with concern.

Artemis just forced a quick smile. "This... this money," she said. "I've never had so much."

"None of us have," Helen replied with an easy laugh. "A hundred million dollars... I mean, half that after taxes I'm sure."

"Tommy said there's a way to hang on to more," Artemis replied, brushing a hand through her dark bangs, her mismatched eyes glancing in the mirror, then darting furtively back to the road again.

Helen gave an easy laugh, tilting her head back. The sun caught her bronze curls, illuminating her sloped features. She'd always been the prettier of the Blythe girls. Everyone had said so, even years ago.

But Artemis had never felt jealous of Helen. She'd only ever felt safe. Felt love.

Things had changed, though. But she hoped they'd change again.

Her family held onto that hope.

Her father had paid the price for Helen's crimes. He'd spent nearly a decade and a half in prison for a crime he hadn't committed, but he'd refused to sell out his own daughter.

Tommy, their brother, had connections with the Seattle mob.

The three of them had been protecting Helen now. Keeping her safe.

Their father had technically escaped from prison, and a manhunt was ongoing.

It was hardly a normal family.

But the hundred million dollars Artemis had earned would go a long way in providing them security, privacy, and legal counsel if ever the need arose.

They weren't just going through the streets admiring the homes.

They were shopping.

For Artemis, this was a drastic change. She wasn't an ostentatious type. She didn't wear makeup, and she didn't often wear jewelry. Her ears were unpierced, and most of her clothing was purchased second-hand or online.

She'd started her career as a chess player, participating in tournaments all across the nation. Recently, things had taken a turn. She'd been involved with helping the FBI as a CI, and chess had taken a backseat.

But now?

Now... she wanted to try again. She'd contacted her analyst friends, the Washingtons, who'd entered her name for an upcoming, online blitz tournament, for that night actually. International tournaments often kept strange hours, but she'd played matches in the early hours of the morning and after sunset before.

The sun dipped below the horizon, casting long shadows over the winding road as Artemis and Helen continued driving through the opulent neighborhood. The dying light flickered in the side mirror, catching Artemis' attention. She squinted at the reflection, noticing a black car trailing behind them.

She frowned, double-checking the license plate, and hesitated.

What might be suspicion or speculation for other people was certainty for Artemis. Her photographic memory took in the plate number, recognizing it immediately.

It was the same car that had been behind them on the highway, fifteen minutes ago.

Her expression flicked into a frown.

"Hey, do you see that car back there?" she asked Helen, trying to keep her voice casual. "It's been following us for a while."

Helen didn't even glance over. She nodded. "Yeah, I spotted it. Figured it was your federal friends."

Artemis' heart skipped a beat. The feds didn't know Helen's involvement in any of it, but it still frightened her to think they were on their tail. Besides, Artemis had heard through the grapevine that someone had been assigned to investigate her family.

She shivered at the thought.

"Maybe," Artemis agreed, though doubt gnawed at her gut. "But I don't like it."

"Let's try to lose them," Helen suggested. "Turn left at the next street. It leads to a forest preserve; we can cut through there."

"Sounds good," Artemis replied, gripping the steering wheel tighter. As they approached the upcoming turn, an icy shiver of fear slithered down her spine. Was this just paranoia? Or was someone truly after them?

"Artemis, breathe," Helen said softly, sensing her sister's anxiety. "We'll be okay."

"Right," Artemis murmured, inhaling deeply as she turned onto the side road. The black car followed suit, its engine revving menacingly.

"Keep going until you see a small dirt path on the right," Helen instructed, her eyes scanning their surroundings. "It should take us deeper into the forest and away from the main roads."

"Got it," Artemis replied, her heart pounding in her chest. Every nerve screamed at her to press harder on the gas pedal, but she knew drawing attention would only put them both in greater danger.

"Here!" Helen pointed to a narrow, nearly invisible path obscured by the thick foliage. Artemis swerved onto it, branches scraping the car's paint as they plunged into the dense woodland.

"Any sign of them?" she asked tensely, her eyes darting back to the side mirror.

"Can't tell," Helen admitted, straining to see through the gloom. "But keep going. The path should lead us out the other side."

As they navigated the treacherous route, Artemis couldn't help but think about their pursuer—and Helen's secret. Was someone after them because of what Helen had done? Guilt weighed on her, suffocating her like a heavy fog.

"Artemis, focus," Helen said, her voice taut with worry. "We're almost there."

"Sorry," she muttered, shaking off her thoughts and concentrating on the road ahead. After several nerve-wracking minutes, Helen said, "Wait! There's a chain blocking the road."

Artemis let out a tense hiss, her knuckles white on the steering wheel. The car idled, its soft purr a vulnerable contrast to the silence that pressed in on all sides. It was then that she saw it—a glint of metal, barely visible in the weak strands of light creeping through thick foliage.

"Stay here," Helen said, her voice low and steady. Without waiting for a response, she leaped from the car, her movements swift and graceful despite the danger they faced.

Artemis watched as Helen approached the chain, her sister's determination evident even in the dark. She marveled at the change in her sibling; once fragile, now fierce. How could this be the same person who had taken lives without remorse?

"Okay, go!" Helen shouted, having unhooked the chain effortlessly. Artemis didn't hesitate, pressing down on the accelerator and propelling the car forward. The tires screeched against the asphalt, a wailing protest that echoed through the night.

"Come on, come on," Artemis urged, her breaths coming in short, shallow bursts. She glanced in the rearview mirror, half expecting to see the car that had been tailing them earlier. But there was only darkness. Had they really lost their pursuer?

"Good job," Helen said as she climbed back into the car, her face flushed with exertion. "Now let's get out of here."

"Do you think they're still following us?" Artemis asked, her voice trembling despite her best efforts to remain calm.

"Hard to say," Helen admitted, her fingers drumming nervously against the door handle. "But we've bought ourselves some time, at least."

"Thanks to you," Artemis said, forcing a smile. The thought of her sister's resourcefulness both comforted and terrified her. How much more damage could Helen cause if she embraced her darker side?

"Whatever it takes," Helen replied, her eyes filled with a steely resolve. "We're in this together, remember?"

"Always," Artemis whispered, the word now a solemn vow rather than a simple affirmation.

The car's tires screeched as Artemis accelerated around a sharp bend, the engine growling like a wild beast desperate for freedom.

Just as Artemis began to feel the weight of her worries lighten, her phone rang, shattering the fragile peace that had settled over them. She glanced at the screen, her heart skipping a beat when she saw Cameron Forester's name flash before her eyes.

"Hey, Cameron," she said cautiously, her voice tinged with curiosity. "What's up?"

"Hey Checkers," the teasing tone of Agent Forester echoed through the phone. She rolled her eyes. "How's it hanging?"

"It's hanging," she said.

"Spend any of that cash yet?" he said.

"Not yet."

"Tragic. Hey, we've got something. You oughta come in."

Artemis frowned. "A case?"

"Mhmm. You really oughta come in."

There was something in his voice that sent shivers up her spine.

"Cameron, what is it? What's wrong?"

"Just... come in, Checkers. And be quick."

He hung up.

She stared at the phone, frowning.

"Is everything alright?" Helen asked.

Artemis shot her sister a quick look. She paused, hesitated, then flashed a smile. "Yeah. Yeah, everything's fine. I just have to head in to work for a little bit."

"I see. Want company?"

"I... to the..." Artemis trailed off, frowning.

Helen smiled. "I've been cooped up for so long. It might be nice..."

Helen had killed an FBI agent. She was wanted by the federals. This version of Helen looked different than the Ghost Killer. This Helen was sweet, smart, prim and proper.

It was unlikely anyone at the bureau would even know who she was. They'd never had a clear picture of her. Especially not how she looked now...

But still... It was risky.

"I can't stay cooped up forever, Artemis," Helen said quietly. "You're my sister. I'd like to go with you. If you'll let me."

Artemis bit her lip. She wanted to refuse. She knew it was what her father would've wanted. But she also couldn't shake the feeling that things had changed for them now. The money provided some assurance, but more than that...

Helen was herself again.

It had been weeks since she'd had an episode.

Besides, Helen was right. She couldn't stay cooped up forever.

"If you stay in the car. Deal?"

"Deal," Helen said happily in that effervescent, airy way of speaking she had.

Artemis nodded, put the car in gear, and pulled away again. She wondered who'd been following them.

Wondered if the FBI was still investigating her. She wondered, also, if the blitz tournament would be as challenging as she thought it might be.

And finally, she wondered what on earth had Agent Forester acting so weird on the phone?

CHAPTER 2

Artemis pulled into the alley behind the warehouse, facing a macabre scene that sent shivers along her back.

She eyed the police cars blocking the entrance to the alley, the sound of hushed voices murmuring from the police officers standing idly by crime scene tape, preventing looky-loos from getting an eyeful.

Her window was rolled down, and she immediately realized this was a mistake. The stench of the alley hit Artemis, the odor of decay and filth seeping into her lungs.

She glanced back at Helen in the rearview mirror; her sister's face was a mask of concentration as she worked on a sudoku puzzle. Artemis hesitated, wondering if bringing her here was the right choice.

"Hey," she said softly, catching Helen's attention. "You sure you're okay waiting here?"

Helen looked up from her puzzle and offered a reassuring smile. "I'm fine, Artemis. I promise."

"Okay." Artemis tried to push her unease aside. One thing at a time, she reminded herself. With a deep breath, she opened the car door and stepped out into the warm afternoon.

The alley was dimly lit, cast in shadow by the large warehouses on either side. A bright floodlight on the ceiling above was dying; like the fluttering wings of an ailing bird, it flickered as it struggled to retain its last bit of life. Shadows danced across the tall warehouse walls, casting eerie patterns that seemed almost alive. Artemis' eyes were drawn to the wooden platform suspended from the wall, an ominous presence looming over the scene below.

Artemis shivered as she approached the crime scene, feeling the weight of her responsibility heavy on her shoulders. Her mismatched eyes—one blue like moonlit frost, the other hazel gold—darted between the evidence, searching for answers hidden in the darkness.

She had to keep up appearances, of course.

The closer she was to the FBI, the easier it would be to keep her ear to the ground in regard to her father and sister. But it was a dangerous game.

Still, solving cases, to Artemis, was much like her sister's sudoku puzzle. It challenged the mind, and it kept her apprised of the FBI's movements.

She knew someone was investigating her.

She also knew that if anyone found out about her father... her sister... their entire family would collapse.

Never before had the bright yellow letters across blue jackets, FBI, been such ominous symbols.

She searched the mouth of the alley, looking for the only friendly face.

She felt a flutter of relief in her chest as her eyes landed on a lanky silhouette by the mouth of the alley.

Agent Cameron Forester, a tall man in a half-buttoned suit, stood under the platform with his arms crossed. The tattoo just visible past the collar of his shirt, creeping up under his neck, hinted at a wild side that clashed with his paltry attempt at a professional demeanor. As Artemis approached, he caught her eye and offered a small wink.

"Hey," he said. "Nice of you to stop by."

The tone from earlier was gone. But she could still see it in his eyes. Something troubling. Something he wasn't telling her, hidden behind that dark gaze.

Forester didn't display emotion like most. As a self-proclaimed sociopath, he found it difficult to empathize. Though, with Artemis... things were somehow different. She couldn't say exactly why, but the two of them were something of an item.

Maybe even more than that.

"So what's this about?" Artemis asked quietly.

"Oh, you know. The usual."

"I don't know. You sounded worried on the phone."

"I did? Huh."

He evaded the question as his gaze returned to the scene before them, his dark eyes scanning the area with practiced precision. "You don't know Jessica Parker, do you?"

"No. Should I?"

"It's our vic." He nodded towards a silhouette laying on the ground.

29

Artemis followed Forester's gaze to the body lying beneath the wooden platform. Jessica Parker, a young woman with auburn hair splayed out around her head like a halo, seemed almost peaceful in death. Beside her, a silver knife glinted in the faint light, its blade stained a dark crimson. Her hands were stained with blood, her neck as well.

"Slit her own throat," Forester said. He shook his head side-to-side, his sandy hair flopping back and forth. The scraggly strands were always unkempt, which matched his misbuttoned suit and mismatched socks, visible just beneath the hem of his trousers.

Artemis stepped forward all of a sudden, brushing against him. "Good to see you again," she murmured. She was refusing to look at the body. "You sounded concerned on the phone," she repeated.

"It's... probably nothing," he said with a shrug. "Just... figured you could help on this one. Where's Helen?"

Artemis' heart skipped a beat at the mention of her sister's name.

Forester knew everything though. The two of them had shared their darkest secrets.

She trusted him. Despite everything, she trusted him with not only her life but her sister's life.

Still, to have him speak Helen's name so casually...

She glanced towards where two cops stood in the mouth of the alley, then returned her attention to the dusty, alley floor.

"She's in the car. Working on a puzzle."

A grunt. Forester then bent down, dropping to a knee. "Got a puzzle of our own."

"So what exactly happened?"

"A couple was walking by last night. They didn't report it until this morning."

"Why the delay?"

Forester shrugged. "Shock. Fear. Dunno. We can ask them though. They're waiting back at the station."

"So what did they see?"

"Not clear on the details yet. But they said this woman here gave some sort of performance, a monologue or something, then slit her own throat. Something about a red dot."

"A what?"

"Laser. Like from a rifle."

"So someone forced her to kill herself?"

"Maybe."

A gust of wind whipped through the alley, sending a shiver down Artemis' spine as she stood next to Forester. The dimly lit space felt oppressive, the tall warehouse walls looming over them like silent sentinels. She glanced back toward her car, where Helen sat patiently with her sudoku puzzle, and shook off her unease.

"Any word on the witnesses' state of mind?" Artemis asked, her voice tight.

"Sober. Coming from a night at the theater," Forester replied, flipping through his notebook. "Like I said, they're being interviewed at the station right now."

Artemis turned her attention back to the scene before her, trying to piece together the events that had led to Jessica Parker's death. As she did, she couldn't shake the feeling that something was amiss. It wasn't just the circumstances surrounding the apparent suicide—something about Forester's behavior seemed off.

She shot him a sidelong glance. He still wasn't meeting her gaze.

She frowned but didn't say anything. Part of her wondered if she ought to mention the car that had been following them...

But if it was an FBI car... she couldn't rule out Forester's involvement. Or even if he wasn't spying on her directly, that didn't mean someone couldn't be using him. No, it wasn't the time for gambits and chances. If Forester wanted to keep secrets, so could she.

Artemis turned away from the body and moved into the side door of the warehouse, frowning as she did.

The puzzle presented itself before her, now. And it was up to her to piece it all together.

Despite Forester's odd behavior, Artemis found there was something calming about solving a case.

It was a type of control she didn't have in her own life. So much uncertainty existed around her.

It was the certain answers she craved most.

And as she stepped further into the warehouse, with a rising sense of relief, she found thoughts of her father, of Helen, of whatever Forester was hiding all dissipated like moisture droplets under direct sunlight.

As Artemis moved away from the doorway, into the warehouse, she took a set of stairs leading to the second floor where the wooden platform jutted out of the side of the building.

She moved slowly, scanning the ground, her eyes searching for any signs of a struggle or tampering. After a few seconds, a glint of metal caught her attention, and she crouched down to examine it further.

"Forester, come look at this," she called out softly, not wanting to disturb the quiet that had settled over the crime scene. She directed her voice through the open window, over the wooden platform.

It took a few seconds, but then she heard his heavy footfalls against the stairs.

A few seconds later, the tall, ex-fighter joined her, scratching at his lumpy, cauliflower ear with a scarred hand. He peered down at the assortment of screwdrivers and screws scattered across the damp pavement.

"Someone put a lot of effort into building that wooden platform," Artemis observed, her lips pursing in thought. "Why go through all this trouble for a suicide?"

"Could be someone wanted to make sure it looked like a stage production," Forester suggested, picking up one of the screwdrivers to examine it more closely. "Or maybe they were just really dedicated to their craft."

As they continued their search, Artemis' eyes were drawn upwards toward the other roof of the opposite building. A cheap, bright light was attached to a metal fixture, casting an eerie pallor over the scene below. Beside it lay something else.

"See that," she said, pointing across the gap between the buildings.

"Mhmm. Like I said. Not a rifle."

She stared at the item. A small pen laser, seemingly discarded in haste, lay under the light-fixture. An image of Tommy as a little boy came to mind, and Artemis could picture him in the lighting booth during her father's mentalism shows, drawing on the backs of people's heads with a little laser pointer just like this one when Helen wasn't looking.

"Seems like someone wanted a very specific lighting setup for this little performance," she mused.

Forester grunted. And again, he struck her as distracted.

Artemis took a few steps towards the window, peering down at the old, worn wooden pallet used as the makeshift stage.

It was stained with blood.

She looked away, further back, into the dark room of the musty warehouse, her eyes attentive, looking for any piece of information that stood out.

Her mind could take snapshot images of scenes. And later, she could recall precise details.

It was both a gift and a challenge.

Sometimes... she remembered things she wished she could forget.

Like the expression on Jamie Kramer's face when she'd chosen her sister over her childhood sweetheart. A pang of regret and longing jolted through her, and she turned away from the window, moving further into the dark warehouse.

She paused suddenly, staring at the ground.

"What is it?" Forester called out, noting her change in posture.

Artemis crouched, examining the ground near the back wall. The concrete was worn and cracked, but she could discern three distinct indentations in a triangular pattern.

Artemis called out, her voice steady despite her racing heart. "Come take a look at this."

He moved to her side, his brow furrowed as he examined the markings.

"Tripod," he said.

"Looks like."

"Camera?" he said.

"Think about it," she said, tapping her finger against her lips. "The wooden platform, the bright light, the pen laser... It's all very calculated. It's as if they staged this entire scene as some sort of production. And you did say that couple had just been to the theater."

"You don't think they had anything to do with it, do you?"

"I'm not sure." Artemis stood to her feet, glancing at Cameron. "Might be good to chat with them, though."

Forester gave a quick nod.

He paused, reaching out and catching her arm before she turned to leave.

She glanced down at his worn, calloused fingers. Fingers of a fighter from another life. Forester had spent a large portion of his youth in a cage, beating people up for a living.

Now though, there was a tender look in his gaze that belied his past occupation.

"Yes?" she said cautiously.

He hesitated and bit his lip. "There's... something..."

She waited.

He let out a long breath. "You know what... later. Let's chat later."

She smiled and gave him a quick kiss on the cheek. He returned the favor by drawing her close and planting one on the top of her head.

Then, at the sound of more footsteps from forensic techs on the stairs, the two of them quickly extricated themselves, cleared their throats, and hastened away from the tripod markings.

"They'll be tired," Forester said, "but I can get them to stick around a bit longer."

Artemis nodded. "I'd like to know why they waited to report the crime until morning."

"Me too," Forester said, frowning. "You don't really think they were involved, do you?"

Artemis shrugged. "Fear makes people act in strange ways. The only question is, are they afraid of something they saw... or something they *didn't* see."

CHAPTER 3

The interrogation room was small and sterile, the air stale and heavy. The single fluorescent light flickered overhead, casting stark shadows against the eggshell white walls. An old, metal table stood in the center, surrounded by four mismatched chairs. The only sound was that of the analog clock ticking ominously on the wall.

Artemis sat rigidly, her fingers drumming an impatient rhythm on the cold tabletop. She kept glancing in the reflective glass across the table, studying her reflection. Her hair, neat and pulled back in a simple ponytail, framed her unique, mismatched eyes.

The thoughts had returned due to the upcoming blitz tournament. Due to the international host, her match would be late this evening. It wasn't much time to prepare, and her time away from the board had her feeling more than a little rusty.

The streaming platform required a video feed. It was the first time she'd be publicly showing her face for quite some time. The first time since she'd joined the FBI. The first time since she'd been framed then cleared of the murder of a fellow chess master. The first time since her father's escape from prison.

Nervous. The word felt wholly insufficient, but she could think of no other better suited to the task. Artemis Blythe felt nervous.

Agent Cameron Forester leaned back in his chair, one leg crossed over the other, looking far too casual for the situation. Artemis studied him from the corner of her eye. Tall and freewheeling, his carefree attitude came forth as he addressed the two timid figures across from them. Emma and James O'Malley. A young, married couple who'd been the one to report the body this morning.

Emma was pretty, and despite the urgency of their report, Artemis could see the telltale marks of blush and eye shadow supporting the young woman's natural looks.

Her face was pale, her hands trembling as she clutched onto James' arm. James, on the other hand, was built like a football player, with a thick neck and muscular arms. He looked like he could take care of himself, but his eyes darted around the room nervously.

"Alright," Forester began, straightening his half-buttoned suit jacket, "let's get this show on the road." His voice, much like his demeanor, seemed cavalier and unprofessional, but Artemis knew better than to judge a book by its cover. There was a sharpness lurking beneath his nonchalance.

Forester leaned back in his chair, the metal legs screeching against the linoleum floor. He stretched out his long legs and crossed them at the ankles, a casual smirk playing on his lips as he studied Emma.

"Can you tell us again what you saw last night?" Agent Forester asked, his voice smooth. "James, buddy, I heard you were hesitant to report this little crime of ours. What gives?"

James clenched his fists under the table, his knuckles turning white from the pressure. "I didn't want to get involved," he muttered, avoiding Forester's probing gaze. "I figured someone else would report it."

A single bead of sweat rolled down James's temple, and she could almost hear the gears turning in his head as he deliberated.

"Forgive me for interrupting," Artemis said softly, cutting through the silence like a knife. "But is that really the reason you didn't report the crime last night? Out of certainty someone else would?" She frowned.

Emma's mouth opened then closed, her hesitation palpable. James shifted in his chair, his fingers gripping the edge of the table until his knuckles turned white. He avoided Artemis' piercing stare, focusing instead on a nonexistent speck of dust on the floor.

"Look, we were scared, alright?" he blurted out, his voice cracking under the weight of his fear. "We didn't want to get involved."

Artemis leaned back in her chair, studying James intently. She knew fear when she saw it—and James was practically drowning in it. But what was it about this particular crime that had him so petrified?

"Well, you're here now," Forester said. "Why don't you give a shot at telling us everything. Leave nothing out."

"Okay," James began, his voice steadier now. He glanced at his young wife, and she fidgeted uncomfortably, adjusting in the metal seat.

"We had just seen this amazing play at the Moore Theatre. You know, the one in the heart of that arts and entertainment district?"

"Love that area," Forester chimed in.

"Right," James continued, nodding. "We were walking down the street after the show, just talking about it. There's always something going on in that part of town—street performers, musicians, the works."

"Such a vibrant atmosphere," Emma added, her eyes lighting up at the memory. "It felt like we were part of something bigger, like we were connected to everyone around us."

It seemed an odd thing to mention, but Artemis just nodded.

"Anyway," James said. "We were headed towards the boardwalk when we decided to take a shortcut through an alley."

"Go on," Artemis urged, leaning forward in her seat.

"Alright," James conceded, "but it's not pretty. Once we turned into the alley," James began, his voice low and solemn, "we noticed a wooden platform on the second floor of one of the buildings. There was a figure standing there, barely illuminated by the dim streetlight."

"Jess," Emma added softly, her eyes downcast as if reliving the moment. "That's what she called herself. She looked scared and desperate."

Forester raised an eyebrow, intrigued. "What happened next?"

"Jess started rambling," James said, rubbing the back of his neck. "Confessing to all sorts of things she'd done wrong. It was like she was trying to get everything off her chest before... well, you know."

Emma nodded in agreement. "She told us about sleeping with her sister's boyfriend, stealing money from her mother, all kinds of messed up stuff. We didn't know what to make of it at first, but we could tell she was genuinely terrified."

"Did she say why she was confessing all of this to you?" Forester asked, leaning back in his chair, his interest piqued.

"Look, I don't know why she chose us to unload all her dirty laundry on," James said defensively, clearly uneasy with the memory. "But it was obvious she was scared out of her mind. We just stood there, listening, not knowing what else to do."

Artemis studied James and Emma's faces, searching for any signs of deception or doubt. But all she saw was the haunted look in their eyes – the unmistakable mark of people who had witnessed something they couldn't quite comprehend. And as she tried to make sense of it all, she couldn't shake the feeling that there was more to Jess' story than met the eye.

"So when did she off herself," Forester said.

Emma shivered. James shot an irritated look at Cameron. "She just pulled a knife... and... and did it."

"Why?" Forester said, leaning in suddenly.

James looked startled.

There was a look in Cameron's eyes that hadn't been there before, a sort of wolfish, lupine stare. One moment, he'd seemed calm, almost indifferent.

But now he looked like a predator with the scent of prey.

"Why did she kill herself?"

"I don't know!" James protested.

"Think!"

"I don't—"

"The red light!" Emma exclaimed. "There was a red dot on her. Like... a laser. Some sort of laser."

"From a rifle!" James said.

"Did you see a rifle?" Forester interjected.

"Yes!"

"No!" Emma corrected. "We just saw the laser. She was very scared, though. We knew that much."

Artemis stood now, frowning across the table. This wasn't adding up. Even if Jessica believed there was a gun trained on her, why would that coerce her to commit suicide? 'Kill yourself or I'll kill you' is an insane threat to make against someone.

"Did Jess look like she was trying to escape?" Artemis asked carefully.

"No," James said. "It was like she was resigned to her fate."

"I see."

"It was all like something out of a movie," Emma said.

Artemis' brow furrowed. "You know, I was thinking the same thing." Forester shot her a look, but Artemis just shrugged. She held up a finger as if to say one moment and then moved towards the door, walking fast.

An idea had occurred to her.

It was almost exactly like a movie. With a tripod and everything.

So what if it was a movie.

She stepped out into the hall, moving quickly. First, she'd check on Helen in the car.

Then...

Then she'd find out if someone had filmed the entire thing.

CHAPTER 4

The car's engine hummed softly as Artemis and Helen drove aimlessly through the city streets.

Helen was at the wheel this time, and Artemis sat in the backseat, her fingers flying over her keyboard as she searched the more unsavory parts of the web. Snuff films. 'Murder porn'. For people who cared to look, there was no shortage of evidence for every kind of evil people were capable of.

It was a distasteful job.

But the hunch was still there, niggling at her mind.

Someone had built the victim a stage. Yes, Emma and James might be considered an audience, but they just stumbled in. Whoever orchestrated this wouldn't risk their work going to waste. If the whole thing had been *filmed*... if it had been set up as some sort of gruesome performance art... Then it would've been filmed. The imprints of a tripod they'd found suggested as much, and the comment the witness had made at the end of the interrogation had only confirmed her intuition.

It was like some sort of bad movie.

And now she was looking for this movie.

She swiped on her phone, searching through the usual suspects—nasty sites on the internet full of the sorts of things that made hair curl.

Artemis didn't visit these portions of the internet, but she knew about them from her time as an online chess streamer. Behind the mask of anonymity, some people revel in the chance to throw disturbing links into humming chatrooms, if only to see how many people they can get a reaction from before they're banned.

Helen kept glancing at Artemis, and Artemis could feel her sister's soft, affectionate gaze fixated on her in the rearview mirror.

The dashboard cast a warm glow over their faces, illuminating the similar features that spoke of their kinship. Artemis glanced at her sister from time to time, her mismatched eyes filled with concern, but it was a quiet understanding that passed between them in those stolen glances.

"Artemis," Helen said, breaking the silence that had settled in the car like a thick fog, "Are you sure there's a film?"

"I... I don't know. But I think someone filmed it. They wanted it seen, so why wouldn't it be uploaded?"

Helen nodded slowly.

"Someone, somewhere must have posted it online. I just need to find it." Her fingers danced across the screen of her phone, searching for any traces of the video that could lead them closer to the truth about Jessica's murder.

As the minutes ticked by, Artemis combed through countless websites, forums, and chat rooms, seeking any mention or clue that could lead her to the elusive film.

The sun dipped below the horizon, casting long shadows across the empty streets. The car's engine hummed softly, providing a comforting background noise.

Artemis frowned as another potential lead turned up nothing. She could feel her frustration growing.

"Artemis," Helen began, her voice hesitant but resolute, "Do you mind if I suggest something?"

Artemis blinked.

What a novel idea... how often had she considered Helen's advice over the years. One enemy at a time. Fear is the threat. Small nuggets of wisdom and tactical advice Helen had imparted chirped in Artemis' mind.

In many ways, Helen was Moriarty to Artemis' Sherlock. The older, smarter sibling, though the young one was in the limelight.

The idea of having Helen on her side, helping to solve the case was somehow... puzzling to Artemis.

But the more she thought about it, the more exciting the prospect was.

"Yeah. Please," Artemis said quickly.

"What about contacting Tommy? He has connections in... certain circles." She glanced nervously at her sister, gauging her reaction.

Artemis frowned, considering the suggestion. Her brother wasn't someone she particularly enjoyed dealing with, but she couldn't deny his resourcefulness. His connections often proved invaluable, especially when handling less savory tasks. "Fine," she acquiesced. "Let's see what he can do for us."

Artemis tapped out a quick message to Tommy on her phone, requesting his assistance. Within moments, the device buzzed with a response, and she activated the speakerphone.

"Hey, sis. Lovely to hear from you. A bit busy at the moment, soooo—"

"Tommy, don't hang up."

A long-suffering sigh filtered back to Artemis over the line, then a hiss and what sounded like a far-off door slamming—or perhaps a gunshot. "Ok—ok. But cut to the chase, Art," Tommy's voice was curt, his usual warmth somewhat more lacking. "I'm... busy."

"Tommy, we're looking for a film," Artemis explained, her tone equally brisk. "A record of a murder. We've tried all the usual places, but it's well hidden. We need your help to find it."

"From who?"

He didn't even question the request. As if it was run-of-the-mill to search for murder videos online.

"I don't know who. It's just... out there. Somewhere."

"A random video online? Needle in a haystack, sis."

"Any advice would be helpful."

A sigh. A grunt. "Try the dark web," Tommy said without pre-amble. "There's a site called 'ExtremeRegret.' You might find what you're looking for there."

"Thanks, Tommy," Artemis said, her voice tinged with reluctant gratitude. "We owe you one."

"Damn right, you do." Before hanging up, though, he paused. His voice was gentler as he said, "How's Helen?"

"I'm fine, Tommy!" Helen called out from the front seat.

"Good. Just... yeah. Good."

And then he hung up.

Artemis sighed, her fingers already moving to access a browser portal that could enter the dark web. She didn't like being in-debted to Tommy, but she had no choice. The stakes were too high to let pride stand in the way.

As an onion search engine loaded on her screen, she couldn't help but feel a flicker of unease. What lay waiting for them within the depths of this digital underworld?

"Alright, let's see what we can find," Artemis whispered to her-self, steeling her resolve as she focused on the screen. Her fingers danced across the keyboard, scrolling through the dark corners of ExtremeRegret.

The posts were a mixture of disturbing images, videos, and text confessions—things that sent shivers down her spine and made her question humanity's capacity for darkness. But she couldn't afford to be bogged down by every unsettling detail. She had to keep pushing forward, ignoring the ghastly content.

"Come on, where is it?" she murmured, her voice barely audible above the hum of the car's engine. Helen glanced at her sister, concern etched on her face, but remained silent in support of Artemis' determination.

As post after post blurred together, Artemis' fingers began to tremble ever so slightly, and she clenched her jaw to steady herself. The images that haunted her peripheral vision were nothing compared to the weight of the knowledge that Jessica's death was out there, waiting to be discovered.

"Why don't you search by date added," Helen said.

"Right, of course." Artemis frowned. She would've normally thought of that. Wouldn't she have? She felt as if she were distracted.

Artemis huffed as she re-ordered the search results.

A sudden surge of relief washed over Artemis as her fingers froze on the trackpad. There, amidst the chaos of ExtremeRegret, was a thumbnail that made her heart skip a beat. The image showed Jessica, her eyes wide with terror, mouth agape in a silent scream.

"Found it," she whispered, the words barely escaping her lips. She looked up at Helen, whose hands were pale from gripping the steering wheel so tightly. "Pull over."

Helen's eyes darted to the side mirror, searching for a suitable place to stop. The tension hung heavy in the air, like the charged silence before a summer storm.

As soon as the car came to a halt on the shoulder, Artemis exhaled sharply, not realizing she'd been holding her breath. Her hand shook slightly as she moved her finger over the video, her mind racing with a mix of dread and determination. There was something sanitizing about a mouse cursor that she missed in that moment. Her finger's proximity to the horror just seemed too close.

"Are you sure about this?" Helen asked.

Artemis hesitated, her finger hovering over the play button. She weighed the consequences of watching the gruesome scene against the burning need to find answers. With a deep, steadying breath, she nodded.

"Jessica deserves justice," she said, her voice firm but laced with sorrow. "And we're the ones who can help bring her killer to light."

Artemis eyed the thumbnail of the video with apprehension. It was as if the dark corners of the image taunted her, daring them to unveil the horror that lay hidden beneath the play button.

Artemis glanced at her sister's pale face, feeling a pang of concern in her chest. Would seeing something like this trigger Helen? She was doing so well... Artemis didn't want to compromise that. "You don't have to watch it, Helen," she said, her protective instincts flaring up. "I can do it on my own."

"No," Helen replied firmly. "I'm fine, Artemis. Really. I want to help. I'm tired of feeling like an invalid." Her eyes flashed. "After everything I did..." She bit her lip. "Everyone I hurt..." She held back a sudden sob but sniffed and cleared her throat as if she refused to give herself the satisfaction of tears in the form of penance. Instead, she said, "I want to help them. To help stop people... like me."

"Not like you!" Artemis retorted. "Don't say that. It's not you. It never was!"

Helen just sighed.

"Alright, but promise me you'll look away if it gets too much?" Artemis insisted, her hazel eye meeting Helen's gaze while the blue one seemed to delve into her very soul.

"Promise," Helen agreed, swallowing the lump in her throat.

Together, they turned their attention back to the screen, Artemis' fingers hovering over the video, her heart pounding wildly. In that moment, the weight of their decision seemed to press down on them like a crushing wave, threatening to carry them out to sea. But underneath the fear and trepidation, a spark of courage burned brightly.

"Here goes nothing," Artemis muttered, clicking the play button.

As the video began, the sisters braced themselves.

Artemis exhaled a shaky breath, the air heavy with unspoken fears and concerns. The screen flickered to life, casting an eerie glow over their faces as they leaned in, eyes focused intently on the grainy footage before them, the phone set on the arm rest of the front seat, allowing Artemis to lean forward and Helen to glance to the side.

They both watched as the scene unfolded exactly as the two witnesses had claimed.

Jessica on a wooden pallet, speaking out. Her voice was muffled. Then a knife. Then a scream.

Then a body plummeting over the edge.

It all happened so quickly; Artemis felt as if she'd built it up in her mind well past the reality.

She played the video again. And again, frowning as the grainy footage showed exactly what the two witnesses had described.

"Wait," Helen breathed, her finger extending towards the screen, her voice an urgent hush. "There, in the glass across the street."

Artemis squinted, following her sister's direction. A reflection shimmered in the windowpane, distorted by the condensation-streaked glass but unmistakable. Her heart raced, pounding furiously against her ribcage as her mind tried to process what she was seeing.

A hooded figure, standing by the glow of the camera lens.

"Someone else was there," Helen murmured, her voice hollow with apprehension. "Recording everything."

They paused the video, the image still and haunting on the screen. Artemis' breath caught in her throat as her mind raced to piece together the implications of this discovery.

"Could it be...?" Helen began, her voice faltering.

"Someone behind the camera," Artemis finished for her, the weight of their words settling over them like a suffocating blanket. "Whoever that is, he's the killer. Whoever standing back... he's the one who did this." She glanced at her sister.

"I'm alright," Helen said, anticipating the question. "Really. I'm fine."

"I wasn't going to ask that."

"Sure you weren't." Helen's cheeks dimpled in amusement.

"Just... nice find. You're good at this."

Helen smiled. "Maybe next crime scene I won't have to wait in the car."

"Really? You don't... don't mind?"

"I know you're scared, Artemis." Helen reached back, placing her hand gently on her sister's arm. "Scared the FBI will figure out who I am. What I've done."

"No... No, nothing like that."

A chuckle. "You can lie to everyone else, sis. Not to me."

Artemis let out a reluctant sigh, then flashed a rueful smile. "I mean... It's life and death, Helen. It's... your freedom. All of ours."

"I can't live cooped up. I can be useful. Like just now. I want to have the chance to help, Artemis. To undo some of the wron gs..." She trailed off, and grief flashed across her face. "I know I can't undo it. I can't make it right." She shrugged. "And maybe I'm ultimately hell-bound, but I'd like to try to help. It would at the very least ease my conscience." She went quiet as she said it, frowning, her brow furrowing as if tackling a difficult math problem. "Is that selfish of me?" she whispered.

Watching her sister's torment ate at Artemis. It was like a burning sensation. But there was nothing she could do to alleviate Helen's pain. As much as she wanted to, there was nothing to do but sit there and listen.

She sighed. "Fine. If you want to help, I don't see why not. Forester won't object. He's... unique."

"He likes you."

"Yeah... Yeah, God help us, I like him too."

The sisters both shared a look and broke out giggling. For a moment, the dreary mood vanished.

But as Helen put the car in gear and Artemis glanced at her phone, her mind returned to the murder on screen.

She pasted the link and sent it via text to Agent Desmond Wade—Forester's partner and a technical genius.

Able to track this poster? she said.

Only a few moments passed before Wade replied. On it.

She settled in the seat, frowning, wondering if the killer knew they were on his trail.

And if so...

Was he still on the hunt? Or was he on the run?

She had a sinking suspicion, that a man who liked spectacle to this degree wasn't the sort to run and hide.

CHAPTER 5

The dim glow of the stage lights cast a warm hue on a man who saw himself as more than just another audience member. He sat in the plush red velvet chair, one leg crossed over the other, a smug smile playing on his lips. To him, he was the director—the mastermind behind every emotion evoked from the performance before him. His fingers drummed rhythmically on the armrest, the beat of his self-importance resonating through the theater.

"Look at that," he whispered loudly to the woman seated beside him, her eyes flicking towards him with mild irritation. "The lead actress is practically drowning in that dress—far too long for her height." He tsk-tsked, shaking his head with a knowing smirk. "I would have chosen something more... elegant."

The woman raised an eyebrow but said nothing, clearly uninterested in discussing it further. She returned her focus to the play, but the man continued, unperturbed.

"Ah, and there's the leading man," he sighed, nodding toward the actor making his entrance. "He's trying too hard to appear confident; it's all very contrived. If I were directing this play, I'd have spent more time coaching him on the subtleties of the character."

"Would you please be quiet?" the woman murmured, her annoyance finally breaking through. "Some of us are trying to enjoy the show."

"Of course, my dear," the man replied condescendingly, leaning back in his seat. "But it's such a pity they couldn't consult someone with real talent."

He smirked to himself, leaning back, and continuing to watch.

But he didn't remain quiet long. The curtains on the stage opened completely now, invitingly. The lights above shone towards the leading man.

"Ah, this scene," the man said, his voice carrying throughout the hushed theater. "It's reminiscent of Shakespeare's *Hamlet*, don't you think?" He gestured grandly with one hand as if unveiling a masterpiece for the audience to behold.

"Shhh!" came a chorus of irritated whispers from all around him like disgruntled snakes hissing in unison.

Unfazed, the man continued, his eyes gleaming with excitement as he leaned toward the woman next to him. "You see, the way the lighting is arranged here—it's quite ingenious, really—creates an atmosphere of tension and foreboding. I've seen similar techniques used in productions of 'Macbeth' and 'Othello.' Of course, I would have added a touch more shadow to deepen the effect." He raised a finger, a triumphant flourish to accentuate his point.

"Please, keep it down," the woman muttered through clenched teeth, her jaw tight with frustration. She shifted away from him in her seat, trying to distance herself from his suffocating presence.

"Fine, fine," the man conceded, waving a dismissive hand. "But it's such a loss..."

As the play unfolded before them, the man couldn't help but compare each detail to other great productions he'd seen or imagined directing himself. The costumes, the set design, the actors' expressions—everything was scrutinized and measured against an invisible scale in his mind. It was as if he was analyzing a symphony, each note dissected and weighed for its worth.

Internally, he scoffed at the mediocrity displayed before him, a running commentary of disdain and superiority playing out in his thoughts. If only the others could recognize his expertise, he mused, the world of theater would be elevated to heights previously unattainable. But alas, they remained ignorant of the genius sitting amongst them.

"Shhh!" a voice snapped again from behind him, jolting him from his reverie. The man's cheeks flushed with indignation, but he said nothing, his wounded ego festering in silence. As the play reached its climax, he clutched at the armrests, his knuckles white with pent-up frustration.

"Bravo! Bravo!" he called out sarcastically as the curtains closed and the audience around him erupted in polite applause. They were all blind to the true potential of the stage, he thought bitterly. But one day, they would see—oh, how they would see.

As the applause around him swelled like a tide of ignorance, the man's frustration and anger turned to bitterness. He couldn't bear the thought that these philistines had the audacity to shush him when he was merely trying to educate them on the finer points of theater. They would rather drown in their own mediocrity than listen to his insightful critiques.

"Can you believe this?" he hissed under his breath to the woman beside him. She started at his sudden outburst, her eyes wide with surprise. "I mean, really! What a disappointment."

"Please," she whispered, her cheeks flushing with embarrassment. "This isn't the time."

"Isn't it?" he scoffed. "If not now, then when? Must we all pretend this farce was anything more than an insult to our intelligence?"

Her silence only served to stoke the flames of his wounded ego. The final bow of the actors was greeted with a standing ovation, but the man remained seated, his arms crossed defiantly over his chest. A scowl etched itself onto his features, as if daring anyone to challenge his dissent.

"Fine," he muttered, mostly to himself but loud enough for those nearby to hear. "You want to live in blissful ignorance? So be it. I refuse to partake in this charade any longer."

With that, he rose from his chair, all wounded dignity and simmering anger. His abrupt movement drew the attention of those nearest to him, their faces a mix of curiosity and annoyance. He met their gazes, unflinching, as if daring them to say something—anything—about his departure.

"Excuse me," he said sharply, pushing past the knees and feet of those in his row, forcing them to stand and make way for him. Each step was a proclamation of his superiority, each annoyed glance and hushed comment only further evidence that they were all beneath him, incapable of comprehending the true beauty and complexity of the theater.

As he reached the aisle, he cast a final glance back at the still-applauding audience, a sneer curling his lips. "Enjoy your mediocrity," he spat before stalking up the aisle and out of the theater, leaving a trail of offended whispers and muttered insults in his wake.

Outside, the cool night air did little to soothe his bruised pride. He clenched his fists by his sides, his breath coming in short, angry bursts. They would come to regret their dismissal, he vowed silently. They would see what true artistry looked like—and they would remember the man who tried to show them the light.

The man paused, inhaling the scent of rain-soaked concrete as he pulled out his phone. He unlocked the screen and tapped on a video file, his thumb grazing the screen with practiced precision. The footage began to play—the dimly lit room, the terrified victim bound to a chair, the cold glint of a blade reflecting in the shadows.

The victim's voice could be heard pleading through the phone speaker, raw and desperate. The man's lips curled into a sadistic smile as he watched the scene unfold.

"Art," he muttered, his eyes never leaving the screen. "This is true art."

As the knife descended, the man felt a surge of satisfaction course through him. He had orchestrated every detail of the murder with exquisite care, each moment meticulously planned and executed. Here was a performance worthy of his talents, a masterpiece eclipsing the drivel that passed for theater tonight. It was his genius captured on film, undeniable proof of his superiority.

"Ah, the climax," he whispered, savoring the anticipation that built as the victim's screams grew more frantic. "A beautiful thing..."

His heart raced in time with the video, the thrill of the kill flooding his senses once more. The thought that they would die at his hand, their final moments immortalized in his twisted production, filled him with an indescribable elation.

"Bravo!" he exclaimed, raising the phone in a mock toast. "To me, the true master of the stage!"

The night air wrapped around him like a cloak, concealing his dark deeds from the world.

"Next time," he murmured, his eyes alight with a dangerous gleam, "the stage shall be grander, the players more worthy of my skills."

As the last echoes of the victim's screams faded into silence, the man grinned.

The night air, damp and cool, slithered around him as he stood in the shadow of the theater's grand entrance. With a self-satisfied smirk, he tapped on the screen of his phone, launching an app that granted access to the dark corners of the internet. It was here, among the whispers and shadows, that his masterpiece had found an audience.

"Outstanding," one comment read, "a real work of art."

"Chillingly beautiful," another praised. "You've truly captured the essence of fear."

His eyes flicked from one accolade to the next, each word stoking the fire of his ego. He drank them in greedily, savoring their validation like a fine wine. Occasionally, he would pause, thumb hovering over the screen, to deliver his own commentary.

"True," he murmured in response to a particularly glowing review, "the subtlety of my technique is unparalleled."

"Exactly," he agreed with another, "the mise-en-scène is a testament."

As the comments continued, the man's chest swelled with pride, his thoughts swirling in a storm of self-congratulation. His fingers danced across the screen, scrolling through the sea of adoration, hungrily searching for more.

"Can you believe it?" he whispered to himself, his voice barely audible above the distant hum of the city. "All these people – they see it. They understand."

He paused, his gaze locked on a comment that seemed to encapsulate everything he had ever wanted to hear. "A true visionary," it said, "an auteur who has raised the bar for all others." But then... It continued. "Not nearly as good as that new one, though. Did you see it? Here's the link."

He stared, certain he'd misread.

He clicked the link.

And a new video opened.

He stared.

A scene with a woman, standing on a wooden pallet. Then a sudden burst of light. A scream. She started confessing secrets. Dark, dark details, spilling them out into the air for all to see.

So much shame... fear... terror...

It was all so exciting. He gaped—someone else had done this.

Someone had achieved what he'd endeavored to. The lightning was perfect, the framing excellent.

And then the climax.

She stabbed herself.

He stared, stunned, certain he was seeing things. "Farce," he whispered. "All farce."

But no... he watched as she raised the blade, and brought it down, dragging it across her own throat.

He stared, stunned, mouth unhinged.

Someone else had posted a video.

In the comments, he read more adulation. Far, far more.

Someone had even written in the description of the video, a tribute to "the Dirextor".

Dirextor was his name on the dark web. The name he posted his videos under.

Someone was copying him.

No...

His lip curled.

Someone was trying to upstage him. To steal his audience.

Someone else was out there, plagiarizing his life's work.

"No, no, no," he muttered under his breath.

Behind him, the theater doors opened, and the plebians swarmed the streets.

He moved away from them, walking fast, staring at the video on his phone.

Another director. A pretender.

"We'll see about that," he muttered, reading another adoring comment.

He would have to outdo himself.

Dueling directors. Murderers with a mission.

He'd respond in kind. He'd come up with his best production yet.

"Yes," he whispered. "Yes, then we'll see what you do!"

CHAPTER 6

As the sun dipped below the horizon, casting an array of pink and orange hues across the sky, Artemis and Helen arrived at a small, waterfront coffee shop they'd chosen as their place to wait until they received the harrowing report on the dark web poster.

Agent Wade was good at his job, but even Wade took time to uncover purveyors of the dark web.

The lingering scent of salt in the air mixed with the rich aroma of brewing coffee as they found a table near the water's edge. A gentle breeze rustled the nearby faux palm trees, a plastic attempt to spruce up the Seattle coastline, their shadows dancing on the white stone beneath Artemis' feet as she pulled out her chair.

"When's the match?" Helen asked softly, taking a seat opposite Artemis. She tried to speak in a calming tone because Artemis could feel her anxiety rising.

There were only a few hours left until her scheduled match time.

It had been some time since she'd played in any official tournaments.

And the last time, she'd been accused of murdering one of the other participants.

Her name had since been cleared, and she'd been able to return to the game she loved.

But she still wasn't sure how the fans would receive her.

Her nerves were fraying, but she tried to keep them in check.

"Any news from Wade?" Helen prompted. Artemis felt a small flush in her cheeks at her own inability to answer her sister's first question. The fact that her sister had shown pity and moved on told Artemis she might already guess how she was feeling about the match.

"None. Not yet," Artemis replied. "I don't expect we'll hear from Wade until he has something concrete we can follow. He's stoic like that."

"Do you really think the man who posted the video is the same one who recorded it?"

Artemis shrugged. "I don't know." Then, if only to change the subject, she said, hurriedly, "Let's set up the call with Cynthia and Henry."

"The Washingtons, yes?" Helen said. Then, in a lower voice, she added, "Is it true I drugged them?" Her eyes were troubled.

Artemis decided not to answer this particular question. She could picture the image of Jamie Kramer's old home. Could picture the Washingtons laying on the floor.

Drugged by Helen.

Instead, Artemis just shrugged. "I think you have the laptop, right?"

"Sure thing," Helen replied, already pulling out the device and clicking away. As she typed, she glanced at Artemis, taking in her patient expression. Neither sister spoke.

The screen flickered to life, and Helen entered the video site's login info. A second later, the screen revealed the smiling faces of the Washingtons.

"Artemis!" Cynthia exclaimed, her excitement evident in every syllable. "How wonderful to see you!" Helen remained out of the frame, and Artemis was grateful she didn't have to introduce her sister.

"Hi, Cynthia, Henry," Artemis greeted, forcing a smile onto her face despite the anxiety gnawing at her insides. "Where are you guys?"

"A cruise!" Cynthia said with a chortle. She turned the screen, showing the vast ocean behind them serving as a picturesque backdrop.

The sun dipped below the horizon, casting an enchanting mixture of oranges and purples across the sky. The gentle lapping of water provided a soothing soundtrack.

"A cruise?" Artemis said, sounding amused. "Good for you. You deserve it?"

"Oh, I don't know about that," Mrs. Washington said bashfully, her dark features crinkling into a smile. The middle-aged woman leaned over and gave her husband a quick side hug. Then she looked up, her eyes gleaming. "But Artemis... we've had a miracle!"

"Oh?" Artemis said, sounding impressed.

"Yes..." Cynthia's voice dropped low, and she leaned forward, tilting the camera so that it was staring at her pink cardigan. She whispered, "We found money in our account."

Artemis just went quiet. She could feel Helen watching her.

Cynthia expounded, "Henry and I discovered a million-dollar deposit in our bank account, and we can only assume it's a blessing from God."

Artemis' lips curled into a small smile. "Wow," Artemis chimed in, feigning surprise. "That's incredible! You both deserve it."

"Thank you, dear," Cynthia replied, her eyes shining with gratitude. "We asked the bank. Henry even went in, trying to return it. But they said the funds were legally deposited. They said we had a benefactor." Cynthia leaned back now, inhaling the sea breeze where she lounged on the deck of their cruise ship.

Helen's gaze lingered on Artemis as the moon replaced the sun, casting a glow over the waterfront café. The clink of cups and saucers mingled with the murmur of conversation around them, but Helen's focus remained solely on her sister. A million dollars? She mouthed.

Artemis pretended as if she hadn't noticed.

She quickly said, "That's amazing, Cynthia. Truly."

"Yes. Yes, well, I don't mean to boast. We're here to help you dear. We're so glad that everything was cleared up, we should add."

"Never believed you were guilty for a second," Henry added with a nod.

Cynthia bobbed her head in agreement.

"Thank you," Artemis said. "I don't know if you know how much you helped me. Truly, thank you."

"Yes, dear. Any time. After everything you've done. It's the least..." Cynthia trailed off as her husband nudged her. "What?" she said.

Henry pointed at the screen. "She's got a game coming up. Let's focus."

"Always chess, chess, chess with you," snapped Cynthia. "There are more important things in life!"

"I know!" Henry said. "But we're embarrassing the girl!"

Artemis didn't try to deny this. Instead, she changed the subject entirely. "Matthew Armon," Artemis said, turning to Cynthia. "What can you tell me about him?"

Cynthia leaned back in her chair, a thoughtful expression on her face. "He's an aggressive player for sure," she began. "Very tactical. He likes to control the board from the start and put pressure on his opponent."

Artemis nodded, absorbing the information. In her mind's eye, she pictured the chessboard, each piece moving in time with Cynthia's words. Her fingers tapped rhythmically on the table, mimicking the movements she would soon make onscreen.

"Also, watch out for his bishops," Helen chimed in, keeping one eye on Artemis. "He's known to use them in unexpected ways, catching his opponents off guard."

"What's his favorite opening?" Artemis asked.

The Washingtons both paused, and she heard clicking, suggesting they were navigating some document on their computer.

As far as analysts went, they were slower than some. But none were better, nor more reliable. They'd been the first ever to analyze one of her games from years ago when she'd first posted it online.

"His favorite opening," Cynthia began, "is the Sicilian Defense. He likes to play it in both the Accelerated Dragon and Najdorf Variations. He's also known to use the Ruy Lopez, as well as the King's Gambit."

Henry nodded in agreement. "He's been known to use some of Fischer's favorite moves from back in his day," he said. "The 'Fischer-Sozin Attack' is one of his go-to openings when playing White."

"And when playing Black, he likes to employ a variation on the 'Marshall Attack'," Cynthia added.

Artemis could already envision how they would look on the board—the pieces moving like clockwork, each move calculated for maximum effect.

"What about notable games? He's played? Not sure I've heard of him." Artemis asked.

Cynthia smiled knowingly. "Oh, there are many! But perhaps his most famous game was against Grandmaster Boris Spaloky at the London Chess Classic in 2018," she said. "He likes to go deep. The clock doesn't intimidate him."

"Alright. Thank you."

"Here, I'm sending you his annotation from the last tournament," Henry said. "One second."

Suddenly, Artemis' phone chimed. She glanced down, expecting to see a notification from Henry, but it wasn't.

She frowned, certain she was reading it wrong.

"What is it?" Helen murmured from off-camera.

Artemis re-read the notification, and then her eyes widened.

"Artemis!" Cynthia said suddenly. "Artemis, I just got an email."

"I got the same," Artemis said quickly. "About the match?"

"Yes."

"What is it?" Helen repeated.

"The blitz game... it's been moved up. It starts in five minutes."

"Five minutes?!" Helen echoed in disbelief. "But that's hardly any time to prepare!"

"I know," Artemis replied, feeling a sudden surge of panic. She had been relying on the extra time to mentally brace herself for the intense match against Matthew Armon.

"Okay, deep breaths," Helen coached, recognizing Artemis' state of mind. "You've got this, remember?"

Of course, she was right. And yet, Artemis couldn't shake the nagging sense of unease that threatened to derail her focus. She closed her eyes, drawing in slow, deliberate breaths as she sat at the café table, the scent of freshly brewed coffee mingling with the briny aroma of the nearby sea. In, out, in, out—she could feel her pulse steadying, her thoughts beginning to coalesce once more.

"Good, keep breathing," Helen encouraged, her voice soft but steady. "Don't let this throw you off-balance. You're still one of the best players in the world, and you can handle this sudden change."

Artemis opened her eyes, her gaze flickering between the screen displaying her upcoming opponent and the gentle waves lapping at the water's edge. She knew that panicking now would only serve to undermine her chances, and she couldn't afford any missteps.

"Are you alright, dear?" Cynthia was saying.

Artemis flashed a warm smile, though inwardly, she felt frigid. "Fine. Definitely. Just fine. But I think I need to log in."

"Good luck!" Cynthia exclaimed.

Henry was busy trying to wave down a waiter with a tray of drinks.

Artemis gave a quick farewell then logged out before signing into her chess account.

"Alright," she whispered, her fingers hovering over the keyboard as the countdown on the announcement banner ticked away. "I can do this."

"Of course, you can," Helen assured her, offering a supportive smile.

She watched on the screen as her opponent logged in.

She cataloged through the information the Washingtons had provided her.

She watched the small, pixilated board on the screen. In a way, being rushed was a blessing.

She didn't have time to read the stream comments. Didn't have time to tune into the commentators and listen to their opinions.

Five... four...

Helen leaned back.

Two... One.

The game started.

The camera on her computer blinked as the stream went live. She couldn't see her opponent's face, just as he couldn't see hers, but she could see by the little icon by his name that he was logged in and ready as well. The two of them online, neither of them witnessing the other's expressions. Mind against mind.

Her opponent's profile picture showed a chubby young man with an easy, cherubic smile.

Artemis' own profile photo was of a wooden queen.

The first move of the game was like the strike of a match, igniting the tension that crackled in the air between Artemis and her virtual opponent, Matthew Armon. Seagulls cawed overhead as the waves lapped gently at the shore, but Artemis remained laser-focused on the screen in front of her.

"Knight to F3," she murmured, fingers tapping the computer mouse with practiced precision.

Helen looked as if she wanted to offer a final word of reassurance, but the camera was live and she couldn't be anywhere near Artemis' screen.

Artemis nodded, her thoughts racing as she anticipated Armon's response. This was a high-stakes game; one wrong move could cost her everything. As the seconds ticked down, Armon countered with his pawn to D5, prompting Artemis to furrow her brow.

As Artemis moved her knight to C3, her phone vibrated on the table, momentarily breaking her concentration. She glanced down to see a text message from Agent Wade: We've located the poster of the murder videos.

Artemis felt her heart constrict, the implications of this new information settling like a heavy weight in her chest.

Everything alright? Helen mouthed, picking up on the change in Artemis' demeanor.

Her eyes flicking back and forth between the screen and her phone, Artemis subtly pushed it towards Helen so her sister could read the texts.

Then another text message.

Stay where you are. We're coming to you.

Artemis frowned at the notification, and she felt a slow chill crawl down her spine.

She played another move on the screen, and it felt as if more moves were being played. Behind the scenes, hidden from sight but at a rapid pace.

CHAPTER 7

They were about to commence the raid, but all she could think about was that rook she'd missed.

Artemis scowled in the dark, dingy space in the heart of Seattle at midnight.

The damn rook! How had she missed it?

She'd won the game, but it had been a limping win. A quick pivot and the sacrifice of *both* of her own rooks gave Artemis the position she needed. Desperate, reckless, but a win nonetheless. She shook her head, wondering what Helen must've thought.

Her sister was waiting in the car again. But for good reason.

Now, Artemis stood at the very back of a group of six federal agents led by Agent Forester and Agent Wade.

Cameron was scratching at his lumpy, fighter's ear, one hand on his weapon, his eyes on the door ahead. Bright lights illuminated the alleyway. Desmond Wade looking perhaps a bit more like a Pitbull than usual. Artemis could only guess what dark corners of the internet his search had brought him to that would leave an expression like that. A serious face, this time without his usual sunglasses, his compact, muscular build tense with a readiness to break some heads. He stood right behind Cameron, his own weapon clutched tight in a meaty fist, looking like a linebacker about to charge the quarterback.

But the target wasn't a quarterback.

Rather, they were facing the door of Alfred Hughes. AKA ExtremeRegret.

He'd posted the murder video on his dark web address, along with many other distasteful videos.

Forester glanced at the others, holding up a finger, the digit going to the earpiece where Supervising Agent Shauna Grant was giving him instructions.

SA Grant had been the one to tell Artemis to join the raid.

For experience.

Artemis wasn't sure if she was being punished for something, but she knew better than to countermand SA Grant.

Now, she waited in the shadows, back against a concrete wall, wondering what sort of lair they'd be charging into.

She could hear the crackle from the radio in the hand of the agent ahead of her. A beefy man with murder in his eyes. The radio was saying, "Known associates... armed and extremely dangerous. Alfred Hughes likely won't be there alone. It's a late-night poker parlor. Run by the mob."

Artemis shivered. They were about to charge into a criminal organization's late-night gambling hall in the hope of finding their internet poster.

She hoped it didn't all go haywire.

Another crackle on the radio. Artemis—observation only.

Artemis blinked. But felt a swell of relief. She wasn't expected to charge in with everyone else.

Thank goodness.

She nodded, flashing a thumbs up to Cameron, to show she'd heard.

The usually cheerful agent gave her a long look as if making sure she would stay put.

And then, he gave the signal.

The six FBI agents all began to move like a stealthy coil of vapor, slithering through the dark alley, rapidly approaching the closed door.

Footsteps tapped rhythmically against the alley floor. Artemis watched from her position of observation. Her eyes moved to a small, gleam that caught her eye along the side of the alley, over a window with a grate.

A security camera.

Had it spotted the FBI agents?

She winced, opening her mouth to call out to Forester, but she didn't want to alert anyone.

Desmond went first, leading with his foot into the door set in the alley wall.

The door splintered open, and the agents charged in.

Artemis couldn't see past them, but she could hear the commotion from inside.

Voices shouting, furniture being overturned, glass shattering.

It wasn't long until Artemis heard someone yell out, "Where's Hughes! On the ground! Where's Alfred Hughes!"

She heard gunshots. Then silence.

And then she heard a noise.

She turned sharply, peering along the side of the alley.

A man was clambering through the window she'd seen earlier. The grate had lifted on rusted hinges.

It squeaked and rattled along with the sound of the man's heavy breathing.

Sure enough, Alfred Hughes was climbing out of it, his compact and athletic build making it easy for him to shimmy down the grate and drop onto the ground below.

He took off running down the alleyway, away from where Artemis was standing.

He shot a glance back at her, and she glimpsed ferrety eyes in a panicked expression.

For a moment, it reminded her of the game she'd just played. She'd sacrificed a rook but won the game. Alfred was prepared to make his own sacrifice, to leave it all behind, escaping with nothing but his life.

Sometimes, even when the unexpected occurred, she had to think laterally.

She cursed under her breath, then broke into a dead sprint, racing after Alfred Hughes down the dark alley. She'd only taken a few paces, though, when she heard footsteps behind her.

She whirled around and gaped.

Helen.

Her sister had emerged from the car she'd parked three blocks away and was now chasing after Artemis.

Artemis paused briefly, shooing at Helen. "No!" she whispered. "Go back! Go away!"

But Helen refused to listen, shaking her head fiercely. "I'm not letting you go after him alone!" she called out.

And then she breezed past Artemis, racing like a gazelle through the dark.

Artemis huffed in frustration but took off again.

The two sisters raced after the fleeing form of Hughes.

For a brief moment, Artemis offered a small prayer that her brother, Tommy, hadn't been involved in this particular outfit.

He had connections to the Seattle mob, but he was more of a lone wolf.

Still, she worried about him.

The thought struck her as somewhat humorous, given that she was now the one—at her older sister's side—sprinting down a dark alley in pursuit of a criminal.

Helen was fast. Far faster than Artemis remembered from their youth.

Ahead of them, the suspect was now reaching a fire escape, gasping as he began clambering up the rusted, metal rungs.

Neither Artemis nor Helen had guns. But it didn't seem like Hughes did, either.

They continued the chase, reaching the base of the fire escape.

Helen clambered up first, then Artemis.

The metal was cold and slippery, and Artemis' fingers ached from gripping it so tightly as she pulled herself up.

Soon, they were on the roof of the building, and Hughes was ahead of them, moving across the compact rooftops as if he'd plotted the escape route before.

They kept running, leaping over air conditioning units and ducking beneath pipes that snaked their way across the rooftop.

The wind picked up, whipping through their hair as they gave chase.

Hughes had a head start but he was still in sight when he rounded another corner.

The two women paused for a moment to catch their breath before deciding what to do next. That's when they heard a noise coming from behind them. It sounded like someone shuffling around in one of the nearby air vents.

Helen frowned, holding a finger to her lips, and moving towards the opening of the vent to investigate.

Artemis waited patiently, watching her sister.

And then she heard the clattering sound of metal.

She whirled around. A figure burst from a vent behind her, having hidden just out of sight. He lunged at her, fingers scrambling for her throat.

But Artemis had been training with her boyfriend.

Agent Forester didn't exactly train to fight nice. He trained to fight dirty, and so Artemis' instincts kicked in.

More specifically, she kicked him between the legs.

Hughes let out a leaking sound like a whoopee cushion as he dropped to the roof.

Helen yelled, scurrying back around the side of the vent.

She stared at where Hughes was moaning, clutching himself and rolling side to side.

Helen blinked. "Nice shot," she said breathlessly.

Artemis felt sick to her stomach but nodded.

At the same time, she studied her sister, stepping back from Hughes.

She'd been scared all of this excitement might trigger an episode from Helen. Might give rise to her darker side.

But Helen looked as placid as ever.

The medicine, the time with her family seemed to be helping.

No... not just helping.

It seemed to be truly working.

For the first time in a long time, Artemis felt a flicker of hope. What if her sister was cured?

What if they could be a family again.

"We should take him back down," Helen was saying.

Artemis nodded. She didn't trust herself to speak. The thought about her sister had brought a lump to her throat.

But she quickly managed to suppress it as they wrangled Hughes, pulled him to his feet, though he was groaning, and pushed him along the edge of the roof towards the fire escape.

"Forester!" Artemis was shouting. "Cameron-—we're up here!"

She heard an answering shout which flooded her with relief. A few seconds later, she heard the rapid sound of footfalls against the fire escape as backup was on its way.

Hughes growled under his breath, still looking very much the ferret with close-set eyes and thin features.

He kept glaring at Artemis, sheer malice in his gaze.

She wondered if he wanted to do to her what had been done to Jessica.

But that assumed he was the one they were after, the one behind the murder.

Had there been others?

She shivered, not quite daring to meet those dark eyes, as if fearful that something oily might contaminate her by prolonged contact.

"We know what you did," Helen said under her breath.

"You don't know shit," Hughes snapped.

"We'll see about that," Artemis murmured.

CHAPTER 8

The harsh glare of the overhead fluorescent lights cast a sterile glow over the small interrogation room, leaving no corner untouched by its unyielding brightness. Artemis sat in a nondescript metal chair, her moonlit frost blue eye and hazel gold eye taking in the scene with a practiced calm. Her simple attire and lack of makeup gave no hint of the sharp mind hidden beneath her unassuming appearance.

Agent Cameron Forester paced before Alfred Hughes, his tall frame clad in a half-buttoned suit that seemed to rebel against his free-spirited nature. The edge of a tattoo peeked out from under his collar, further emphasizing his incongruity in this setting. His face was a mask of determination, frustration simmering just below the surface.

"Start talking, Hughes," Forester growled, slamming his hands on the table between them. "We know you posted that murder video on the dark web. What's your connection to ExtremeRegret?"

Hughes shrank back from Forester's imposing presence, his eyes wide with fear. He swallowed hard, sweat trickling down his forehead as he stared at the agent. "I-I don't know what you're talking about," he stammered, his voice cracking under the weight of Forester's demand.

Forester leaned in closer, the intensity in his eyes never wavering. "Don't play dumb with me, Alfred. You think we'd bring you in here if we didn't have evidence? We've traced the video back to you. Now tell me—why did you post it?"

Artemis observed the exchange closely, searching for any clues that might help her understand.

"Look, I don't know anything about that!" Hughes insisted, his voice trembling as he attempted to maintain his composure.

"Mr. Hughes, we know you posted that video. What we don't understand is why," Forester insisted, his tattooed neck tensing as he fought to maintain control over his frustration.

Hughes hesitated, his gaze fixed on the polished metal table before him. The fluorescent lights overhead cast harsh shadows across his sweat-soaked forehead, betraying his fear. He clenched his trembling hands into fists, desperately searching for a way out of this situation. "I... I can't say," he finally whispered, his voice barely audible.

Artemis watched intently, her mind racing as she dissected every word, every gesture, seeking the truth hidden beneath the surface. She knew there was more to this man than met the eye.

"Can't or won't?" Forester challenged, his voice low and threatening. "Because if you're not going to cooperate, we'll make sure everyone knows about your little side gig on the dark web."

Hughes's face paled at the agent's words, his breath catching in his throat. They had him cornered, and he knew it. "No, please..." he begged, his voice wavering. "You don't understand—"

"Then help us understand, Mr. Hughes!" Forester barked. He could play bluster and bravado well enough, but Artemis knew he didn't really mean it. Forester could turn on the wolf-hound. But when he got really dangerous was when he meant it. The n... it was as if something in him changed.

But she knew him well enough now that she could place this particular spectacle as an act. Theater.

Fitting giving the crime scene.

Artemis remained an unwavering observer, her sharp mind cataloging each new piece of information. She could see the cracks forming in Hughes's resolve. She'd been a student of body language ever since her father had taught her to read non-verbals as a child.

The tensing of his hands. The faint swallow. The perspiration. It all added up to a single result.

Hughes would crack.

Forester's knuckles whitened as he clenched the edge of the table. He glanced back, and his expression briefly morphed. He grinned at Artemis and winked.

She resisted the urge to roll her eyes.

But then Cameron turned back around, barking again. "Come on, dammit! Don't make me come across this table!"

Hughes remained silent, his eyes darting around the sterile room as if searching for an escape. Perspiration glistened on his forehead, each bead a testimony to his fear.

"You think you can protect your buddies in the mob by keeping quiet?"

Hughes said nothing, but his trembling hands betrayed the turmoil within him. He bit the inside of his cheek, struggling to maintain a semblance of composure.

It was then that Artemis decided to intervene. Her cool, calculated voice sliced through the tension like a razor, her words carefully chosen. "You know, Mr. Hughes, it's only a matter of time before your mob connections discover your little side gig on the dark web. And when they do, I'm sure they won't be too pleased."

As she spoke, Artemis leaned in closer to Hughes, her mismatched eyes locked onto his like a predator stalking its prey. She could sense the subtle shift in his demeanor, the way his breathing hitched ever so slightly. It was clear that her words had struck a nerve.

"Wh-what are you talking about?" Hughes stammered, desperately trying to feign ignorance. But his fear was palpable, hanging in the air like a heavy fog.

Artemis allowed herself a small, knowing smile. "The truth has a way of coming out, Mr. Hughes. Especially when it involves something as volatile as organized crime. You post those videos... what are the odds you've posted murders online that should've been quiet. That the mob didn't want publicized?

Hmm? How do you think they'll react to finding out you've been making them special."

It was all guesswork, but not really a shot in the dark. More like a direct bullseye on a visible target.

Her words hung heavily in the air, their implications not lost on Hughes. As he grasped for a response, his mind raced with thoughts of retribution from his mob associates, the possibility of losing everything he had worked so hard to build.

Forester, sensing an opening, pressed on. "If you help us now, we might be able to protect you from them. But you need to tell us everything."

Artemis watched as the last of Hughes's resistance crumbled like a sandcastle before a rising tide.

Hughes' eyes darted around the interrogation room, a trapped animal searching for a way out. The sterile walls seemed to be closing in on him as each second ticked by. His voice cracked when he finally spoke, betraying the fear that had settled into his bones. "You don't understand... If they find out I'm talking to you..."

"Then perhaps you should have considered that before dipping your toes into their world," Artemis replied, her voice low and threatening. She leaned even closer to Hughes, her mismatched eyes boring into him like twin lasers. Her cool and calculated demeanor was a stark contrast to the mounting tension in the air.

"Look, I didn't kill anyone!" Hughes blurted out, beads of sweat pooling on his forehead. He knew the mob wouldn't care about his innocence; it was his cooperation with law enforcement that would seal his fate.

Artemis studied him for a moment, her expression unreadable. Then, she leaned back in her chair, crossing her arms over her chest. "You're right, Mr. Hughes. It doesn't matter whether or not you committed the murders. What matters is that you've attracted the attention of people who play for keeps. And now, the only way to save yourself is to tell us everything. Even in prison, you won't be safe from them. You have to know that."

His reaction had confirmed her suspicion. He had posted items online that his contacts in the mob wouldn't appreciate.

However...

It was also concerning. Did it mean there were other things he'd posted from others? If so... was he not the source of the murder video? Who was then?

The air in the room grew heavier, as though the very atmosphere itself was pressing down on them.

Hughes swallowed hard, the reality of his situation sinking in. His hands trembled in his lap, betraying the terror that coursed through him. The room seemed to spin around him, his breathing coming in shallow gasps.

"Please... I just... I need protection," he pleaded, his voice barely audible. "If I talk, they'll kill me."

Artemis leaned forward once more, her eyes locked on his as she nodded slowly. "Then you'd best make sure your information is worth our protection, Mr. Hughes. Because if it isn't..." She let the threat hang in the air, unspoken but unmistakable.

As tension in the room reached a fever pitch, Hughes finally broke, the dam of his silence crumbling under the weight of his fear.

"Alright," he croaked, his voice shaking with fear. "I posted the videos, okay? But I swear, I didn't kill anyone."

His words tumbled out in a desperate rush, as if by speaking faster he could somehow outrun the consequences of his actions. He shrank back in his chair, hands wringing together nervously beneath the table.

"Please, just... just don't let them find out," Hughes begged, casting furtive glances toward the mirrored glass that concealed unknown observers. "You don't know what they'll do to me."

Artemis' eyes never wavered, taking in every stutter and tremble, analyzing each piece of the puzzle that was Alfred Hughes. Her mind raced, calculating the implications of his confession and the likelihood of his involvement in the murders.

"Explain," she demanded, her voice cool and measured. "If you didn't commit the murders, why were you posting the videos?"

Hughes swallowed hard, feeling cornered and exposed. "I... I'm just a middleman. I get the videos from someone else, and I just put them up. I don't ask questions; it's not my job to care about what's in them. It's... just a bit of fun. That's all. A hobby."

He stared down at his trembling hands, unable to meet Artemis' gaze any longer. He tried to distance himself from the horrific content of the videos, focusing on the simple transactions that took place between him and the true perpetrators.

"I don't even watch them," he added, his voice barely a whisper. "I swear."

Artemis studied him for a moment, searching for any sign of deception. She could feel the gears turning in Hughes' mind as he attempted to salvage what was left of his life and reputation.

"Who gives you the videos?" she asked, her voice quiet but firm.

"I don't know," Hughes replied, shaking his head. "It's all anonymous. I never see their face or hear their voice."

He looked up at Artemis, pleading with his eyes for understanding and mercy. "Please, I'm just a pawn in this game. I didn't want any part of it. You have to believe me."

The room seemed to hold its breath, waiting for Artemis' next move.

"Look," Hughes stammered, his chest heaving as if he were struggling to catch his breath. "I couldn't have killed anyone. I wasn't even in the city the past two nights."

"How do you know we're looking at a recent murder?" Cameron said.

"Because you're here, aren't you? I know what I posted. But I wasn't in town."

Artemis raised an eyebrow, her gaze never leaving Hughes' face. She watched as he fumbled in his pocket, extracting a handful of crumpled ticket stubs and tossing them onto the table between them.

"Here, see for yourself," he said, desperation edging his voice. "These are my poker tournament tickets from San Diego. And I've got witnesses who saw me there. You can check with the hotel—they'll have security footage, too."

His words tumbled out like marbles spilling from a jar, each one crashing into the next as he attempted to build a wall of evidence around himself. Artemis picked up one of the ticket stubs, studying it carefully, then returned her attention to Hughes. His eyes darted from her face to the tickets and back again, searching for any sign of doubt or suspicion.

Artemis leaned back in her chair, her left hand idly tapping on the edge of the table. Her mind raced, weighing the evidence before her and considering the implications.

If he wasn't the killer, his involvement with the dark web still made him useful– a potential link in the chain that led to the true perpetrator.

"Alright, Mr. Hughes," Forester said finally, his voice cool and measured. "We'll look into your alibi. But don't think for a moment that this absolves you of your involvement in these activities."

Hughes relaxed. "Who sent you the video of Jessica Parker," Forester demanded.

"Wh-who?"

"The one you posted yesterday. The one of the woman on the wooden platform."

"Oh, shit... that one? I don't have a damn clue."

"Don't lie to me!"

"No, I swear. It's anonymous. No one in the mob. I know that much."

"Hughes... are you lying?"

He whimpered. "NO! I swear!"

Forester was shaking his head in disgust.

Hughes, panicked, exclaimed, "Wait—wait! I don't know who sends them, but I can show you his other videos!"

Artemis and Forester stared. "Other videos?" they said in unison.

"Oh... hell yah. And you think that one's bad? The others are just plain evil."

CHAPTER 9

The inky blackness of the night enveloped the Prodigy like a shroud as he pounded the pavement, his breath coming out in ragged gasps. Each stride was calculated and powerful, propelling him forward with an almost unnatural speed. Sweat trickled down his brow, stinging his eyes, but he didn't care. This was his time—when the world slumbered and he could push himself to the limit, testing the boundaries of his body and mind.

His sneakers struck the ground with a rhythmic beat, echoing through the empty streets. He reveled in the intoxicating blend of pain and adrenaline coursing through his veins. The Prodigy had always believed in his own greatness, that he was meant for something extraordinary, something beyond the mundane existence of those around him. And now, he finally had a tangible goal: to surpass the dirextor, a figure who haunted his thoughts and taunted his ambitions.

He muttered self-affirmation slogans under his breath between strides, steeling himself against the fatigue that threatened to overwhelm him. He couldn't afford to be anything less than exceptional; mediocrity was not a word in his vocabulary. Nor was failure.

As he rounded a corner, a sharp burst of wind whipped through the air, sending chills down his spine. But it only served to invigorate him further. He clenched his fists, driving his arms back and forth with greater force, willing his legs to move faster. His heart thundered in his chest, and he welcomed the sensation – it reminded him that he was alive and capable of extraordinary feats.

"Isn't that right, Dirextor?" he growled to himself, imagining the faceless adversary who had unwittingly become the catalyst for his determination.

His thoughts raced as quickly as his feet, and he couldn't help but feel a surge of excitement at the prospect of triumph. He would not only surpass the poster with the username dirextor but obliterate any doubts about his own capabilities.

The Prodigy's breaths came in harsh gasps as he raced through the shadows of the dimly-lit streets, sweat dripping from his brow. His phone screen cast a cold, blue glow across his face, even as he ran, his eyes scanning the chaos of comments and usernames until they landed on one that made his heart quicken: dirextor.

"Look at you," he muttered under his breath, an odd mix of admiration and envy lacing his words. "Always one step ahead, aren't you?" He studied dirextor's latest dark web video. Dirextor had a gift for storytelling, an uncanny ability to captivate and terrify audiences in equal measure. The Prodigy couldn't deny the allure, but it was more than just the content that drew him in; it was the challenge of surpassing someone who seemed untouchable.

"Time to find my own story," he whispered, his fingers tapping rhythmically on his phone.

He knew his next project had to be bigger and better than the last.

Jessica Parker had raised eyebrows.

But that didn't mean he could stop there.

No... no, the best way forward was to find something that garnered already existing attention.

What were some news stories locally?

His mind moved back, thinking...

And then it struck him.

Of course! It had been in the headlines for weeks now!

"The Ghost Killer..." he mused, repeating the name like a mantra as he recalled the recent news coverage that had transfixed the nation.

"Maybe you're the key," he said softly, his eyes narrowing with determination. He imagined the headlines, the whispers of fear and fascination that would follow. The world would be his captive audience, unable to look away from the twisted tale he would weave.

But how to find the Ghost Killer? Otto Blythe had escaped prison, and no one knew where he was.

He paused, scrolling through the news article with sweaty fingers, slowing his pace a bit so he wouldn't keep jarring and making it difficult to focus on the screen.

And that's when he spotted the recommended news article. Just below Otto Blythe's mugshot.

Ghost Killer's daughter cleared of murder charges! The first sentence read.

He felt a shiver up his spine.

He clicked the link and found himself staring at a pretty face with mismatched eyes.

He read the name under the picture.

Artemis Blythe.

"Hello there," he whispered. "What secrets do you have then, hmm?"

It was the confession of secrets that most allured him to this particular project.

He'd set Jessica up with fear. He'd threatened her family. Had threatened her children. He'd told her the laser was a rifle scope.

She'd been a fool.

But fear was a powerful weapon and so was love.

Out of love for her family, she'd taken her own life. She'd confessed her guilty conscience. It was amazing what a simple act of perceived penance could arouse in humans.

Now, his finger stroked the photograph of Artemis Blythe, and he felt a giddy shiver tremor down his spine.

"Everyone has secrets," he whispered, a wicked smile spreading across his face. "And I'm going to unearth yours, Ms. Blythe."

His heart raced as he envisioned the impact his revelations would have on his growing audience. They craved the darkness he provided, and he would deliver in spades. As he reveled in the thought of surpassing dirextor, he couldn't help but feel a sense of satisfaction at the idea of exploiting Artemis for his own gain. After all, it was art.

He was now walking. He wasn't sure when he'd stopped jogging.

But he was still breathing heavily, still striding through shadows like some wraith.

"Alright," he said, cracking his knuckles and turning his attention to his screen.

He opened up multiple tabs, searching through news articles, social media accounts, and obscure forums in an attempt to glean any information about Artemis Blythe.

"Ms. Blythe," he murmured, his eyes narrowing as he scrolled through countless pages. "Let's see what skeletons you're hiding in your closet."

As he delved into the depths of the internet, the Prodigy became increasingly engrossed in his research.

And then there, he spotted it.

A phone number. Listed on a site for chess analysts. It was an old post...

But still current?

He shrugged to himself, activated his VPN on his phone, which would hide his location, and then placed the call.

He waited, feeling a rising sense of nervous anticipation. Would Artemis Blythe answer?

He felt excitement growing.

The phone rang twice before a soft voice answered on the other end. "Hello?"

The Prodigy's heart leaped in his chest. "Is this Artemis Blythe?"

There was a pause before the voice replied, hesitantly. "Yes, who is this?"

The Prodigy swallowed, trying to steady his voice. "I'm... a journalist. I was hoping to speak with you about your father and the accusations against him."

Another pause, longer this time. "I'm sorry," Artemis said finally. "I can't talk about that right now."

The Prodigy leaned forward, his voice low and urgent. "Please, Ms. Blythe. I believe there's more to your story than what's been reported. I want to help you tell it."

There was a long silence before Artemis spoke again, "What's your name again?"

"Dale Gobert," he said quickly, making up the name on the spot. She was acting nervously. He could hear it in her voice. "Ms. Blythe," he said, "what if I were to tell you, there are those who think you might have had something to do with your father's escape."

It was a shot in the dark. A complete fabrication. Unlikely to be true.

"I'd probably just laugh," the woman replied.

She didn't miss a beat. No hesitation. No fear. Either she was telling the truth, or she was really good.

He felt a flicker of excitement. "Is it possible to meet up?" he said. "I can pay you."

"No. No thank you. Please don't call again."

"Wait!" he said urgently. He was scanning his phone desperately now, searching for anything he might be able to use. Something that might gain her attention.

"What?" she said.

He was reading a news article on his phone even while speaking into the receiver.

And then he read the line, estranged boyfriend, Jamie Kramer...

He blurted out, "Jamie Kramer said you would want to speak."

She went quiet.

He felt another flicker of excitement. He was clearly onto something. Something had her spooked.

He filed the name away. Jamie Kramer.

But then she cleared her throat, "Sorry. I'm not taking interviews."

And then she hung up.

He frowned and tried to dial again, but he went straight to voicemail.

"Shit." She'd blocked his number.

He stomped through the streets, frowning as he did. He had options now. He'd heard the pain in her voice.

Jamie Kramer had wounded her.

This was good.

Very good.

He nodded to himself, breaking into a jog again and starting to run once more.

Arms pumping, legs stretching to their full length.

Secrets couldn't remain buried forever.

He would reveal them to the world and baptize the consecration in blood.

It was art, after all.

CHAPTER 10

It was a testament to the content on the dark web, that the phone call was only Artemis' second creepiest experience in the last half hour.

Artemis stood in the dark break room, illuminated by old vending machines, while staring at her phone, wrinkling her nose.

What an odd call.

She'd never heard of this Dale Gobert, and yet he seemed to know so much.

The name Jamie Kramer had been enough to make her heart twist in pain.

Artemis' thoughts raced, and she felt a cold shiver run down her spine. But she forced her attention to the two others who were standing by the table, staring grimly at the computer screen.

The clock on the wall struck midnight, its echoes reverberating down the quiet hallways of the precinct. Artemis, Forester, and Helen stood in the dimly lit room, their shadows cast along the walls like specters, their breaths held as if the slightest noise would shatter the fragile atmosphere. The tension was palpable, a heavy weight that bore down on them as they prepared to confront the horrors that awaited them.

In the eerie silence, the fluorescent lights overhead flickered fitfully, casting an unsettling strobe effect across the room. Through the thin walls, distant sirens wailed like lost souls, adding to the cacophony of unease that enveloped them. And as the clock continued its relentless march forward, their trepidation only grew.

"Damn these lights," Forester muttered, rubbing his eyes. "Feels like we're in some kind of horror movie."

"Maybe we are," Artemis replied, her voice barely above a whisper. The reflection of the flickering light danced in her mismatched eyes.

Helen shifted nervously, her gaze darting around the room as if searching for some hidden threat lurking in the shadows.

Forester had given her permission to join them, especially since it was off hours for the precinct. "Can we just get this over with?" Her voice trembled.

"Right," Forester nodded. He took a deep breath, steeling himself for the task at hand. "Let's do this."

Forester's fingers flew across the keyboard, his eyes narrowed in concentration as he connected the laptop to a large screen mounted on the wall. With practiced ease, he navigated to the folder labeled 'Downloads from Case #01987' and opened it, revealing a series of video files.

"Here they are; Wade tagged everything the creep gave us," Forester said, his voice strained. "The murder videos. Are you ready for this, Artemis?"

"Ready as I'll ever be," she replied, her voice barely audible as she tried to quell the uneasiness that had settled like a stone in the pit of her stomach. She took a deep breath, bracing herself for the onslaught of terror that awaited them.

The first video began to play, its grainy footage flickering on the screen like some twisted home movie. As the horror unfolded before her, Artemis' heart raced, threatening to burst from her chest. Her eyes darted away from the screen during the most disturbing moments, but she couldn't escape the guttural screams that filled the room, echoing through her very soul.

"Stop!" she cried, unable to bear it any longer. "Please, just... stop."

Forester paused the video, his own face serious but otherwise showing no sign of unease at the gruesome displays. For a fleeting moment, Artemis was both jealous and chilled by the self-diagnosed sociopath's seeming immunity to the cruelty they'd just witnessed. "We don't have to watch them all at once, Artemis," he said gently. "We can take breaks if you need to."

"I know," she whispered, struggling to maintain her composure. "It's just... I've seen death before, but never like this. It's so... intimate. And cruel."

"Unfortunately, that's what we're dealing with here," Forester said, his tone grim. "These killers are sadistic, and they want us to see every gruesome detail of their crimes."

Gritting her teeth, Artemis forced herself to focus on the screen as another grisly scene played out. She noticed something peculiar about the way this video was filmed compared to the others.

Artemis leaned closer to the screen, her unease growing as she observed the dirextor's videos. The footage was undeniably amateurish; shaky camera movements and poor lighting made it difficult to discern details. Yet, this raw, unpolished quality only seemed to amplify the brutality of the murders.

"Look at how the dirextor films these scenes," Artemis commented, her voice barely more than a whisper as she tried to suppress the bile rising in her throat. "It's like they don't care about the aesthetics, only the violence."

Forester nodded, his jaw clenched. "They're focused on the kill itself. And... wait, so is he a director or dirextor?"

She glanced at him. "Both. His username is dirextor. With an x. His occupation is director. A gross director named dirextor."

"I'm confused."

"Just stay with me, big guy."

Forester nodded, tapping his nose and pointing at her. "So... you think the scenes are different than our director dirextor?"

"Wait... okay, now I'm confused... But focus. This set up, those scenes? It wasn't the case with Jessica Parker," Artemis said. "It was staged. Even well-lit." She wrinkled her nose. "Like a production. These videos..." She shook her head. "Less so."

Artemis couldn't help but shudder at the thought. She forced herself to continue watching, hoping to find some clue that would lead them to the dirextor and put an end to this nightmare.

"Yeah... yeah, you're right," Forester said. He clicked over to the video of Jessica Parker again. The wooden pallet, the monologue before the kill.

As the new video played, Artemis immediately noticed the differences. The latest video was disturbingly polished, each scene framed with professional cinematography and precise lighting. The attention to detail was unnerving, transforming the gruesome acts into something horrifyingly intentional.

"Everything is so... calculated," Artemis murmured, her eyes darting between the two sets of videos.

"Exactly," Forester agreed. "While the dirextor's work is chaotic and raw... Look, see." He pointed to a comment feed under the video. "It's a tribute to the dirextor's work, but it's not by the dirextor. This guy who posted it... calls himself the Prodigy." Forester wrinkled his nose.

"So we have two killers," Artemis said, wincing.

"They're competing with each other," Helen added. "At least the Prodigy is. He wants to one-up the others."

Artemis paused, thinking of Helen's own background. She knew about the Professor. Knew about a killer who'd taken Helen under his wing, after a fashion, and then turned on her.

She wondered what it was like for Helen to witness all of this.

And yet her sister had proven again and again, she was back to normal.

Artemis believed this.

She had to believe it.

Forester was saying, "The Prodigy's is deliberate and refined. They've clearly learned from their predecessor and adapted their style accordingly."

Artemis bit her lip, her mind racing as she considered the implications. Both killers were dangerous but in different ways. The dirextor's savagery was fueled by an insatiable bloodlust, while the Prodigy's cold precision indicated a calculating mind.

Artemis stared at the screen, her mismatched eyes narrowing as she processed the information. "You know what this means, right?" she said as she turned to Forester. "These two killers... they know of each other."

"Apparently," Forester replied, his tattoo partially visible as he leaned closer to the screen.

"I mean more than just a passing nod. The Prodigy is very familiar with the dirextor's work. I think that means he's been watching these murder videos for a long while. Maybe he was even initiated by them. Look at the tribute video," Artemis gestured towards the footage playing in front of them. "The Prodigy is mimicking the dirextor's style in some parts but refining it in others. It's like a twisted homage, an acknowledgment of their connection."

"Damn." Forester ran a hand through his hair, visibly frustrated. "We've got two psychos working together, but we can't even track down their usernames. They're encrypted, which means we're back at square one."

"Encryption just means they're smarter than your average killer," Artemis mused, studying the videos once more. "If they've taken precautions to hide their identities online, then maybe we can find something in the raw footage."

"Let's hope so," Forester sighed, rubbing the back of his neck. "I'm tired of chasing shadows."

Artemis watched as the fluorescent lights flickered overhead, casting eerie shadows on the walls. She knew that they had little time to spare, but she couldn't shake the feeling that there was something vital hidden within these videos, a piece of the puzzle that would bring them closer.

"Forester, I want to go through each video again, frame by frame," she said, her voice firm with determination. "Look for anything that could tie them together, locations, weapons, clothing, anything."

"Got it," Forester nodded, his fingers flying across the keyboard as he prepared to scrutinize every second of the chilling footage.

Helen nodded in approval at her sister's comments, but she stood up abruptly. "Do either of you want something to drink?"

"Nah," Forester said.

Artemis just shook her head.

Instead of going to the vending machines in the breakroom, though, Helen moved past them and began hurrying out the door.

Artemis watched her leave, hesitant.

For a moment, Forester's fingers stopped flying over the keys as they both watched Helen leave.

"How's she holding up?" Forester said once Artemis' older sister had vanished down the hall.

"Fine. Really."

"Mhmm."

"Thank you."

She turned to him.

"For what?" He quirked an eyebrow.

"For trusting her."

"I don't," he said simply. "But I trust you."

She shrugged. "Good enough. Thank you," she added, a bit more gently.

He eyed her up and down, turning completely away from the laptop for a second. "You know, you're hot when you're grateful."

"Grateful?" she said. She snickered. It was strange how looking at Cameron temporarily distracted her from the context of their meeting. The laptop was briefly forgotten.

He reached out, pulling her close, his rough hands gentle against the soft skin of her fingers. Leaning down, he kissed her knuckles, his lips grazing her fingers.

"Then again," he said, "I figure you're always hot."

She hid a smile, but glanced nervously at the door, wondering if Helen would return at any moment.

"Cameron! Now's not the time."

He kissed up her arm, slowly, his fingers still touching hers.

Artemis couldn't help but shiver at the sensation of his lips against her skin. She knew they had to focus on the task at hand, but part of her couldn't resist the thrill.

"Cameron, seriously," she whispered, trying to push him away gently. "We need to focus on the case."

He pulled back, his eyes dark with desire. "I know," he said huskily. "But it's been so long since we've had a moment alone. And with your sister here, it's just... "

"I know," Artemis sighed, feeling torn. "But we have to stay professional. We're at work!"

"I know," Cameron repeated, his voice heavy with regret. "I just... damn, Artemis, you drive me crazy."

She smiled, feeling a rush of affection for the man beside her. Despite their differences, they had a deep connection that went beyond their shared passion for solving crimes.

She looked at him for a moment longer then said, softly, "What was it you didn't tell me."

He stared.

"You wanted to tell me something on the phone. Then this afternoon. But you didn't. What was it?"

He stared at her, hesitant.

Then he scratched at his chin. "You know... it's nothing."

She frowned, withdrawing her hand.

"I'll tell you after all of this," he added quickly.

"So there is something?" she asked, leaning one hand against the cool, wooden table. The glow from the vending machines behind her created an eerie aura around them, adding to the tension and the secrecy of their conversation.

Cameron hesitated for a moment, then sighed. "It's just... it's personal. And I don't want to burden you with it right now. We have too much on our plates as it is."

"Personal? Cameron—when has something private ever stopped you from blurting it out loud. In public. Loudly."

He glared at her.

She didn't budge.

"Fair point," he muttered.

"Is it about us? Are you getting cold feet?" Artemis asked, her heart pounding in her chest. Had he changed his mind about their relationship? Had he met someone else?

Cameron shook his head quickly. "No, no, nothing like that. Nothing bad. I promise. It's just... something I've been dealing with. And I don't know how to handle it."

Artemis studied him for a moment longer, then nodded. "Okay. I understand. But if you ever need to talk, you know I'm here for you, right?"

Cameron smiled, his eyes softening. "I know," he said, reaching out to take her hand once more. "And I appreciate it. You're always there for me, in more ways than one."

Artemis blushed, feeling a familiar warmth spread through her body at his touch. She knew they had to be careful, especially with Helen just down the hall, but she couldn't help the way she felt around Cameron.

He made her feel safe.

Her mind wandered to the car that had been following her earlier. If he'd been with them, she wouldn't have felt nearly as scared.

Now, though, Cameron was turning back to the computer.

Artemis leaned in closer to the screen, her mismatched eyes narrowed as she scrutinized the older videos.

It was like plunging back into an icy pool after a warm shower. She stared at the gruesome footage, willing it to end.

One scene after the next. One file after the next.

It was all too much.

"Wait," Artemis whispered, her voice barely audible as she paused the video on a particular frame. "Forester, look at this."

Forester glanced over at the screen, his frustration momentarily forgotten as he tried to discern what Artemis had spotted. "What am I looking for?" he asked, his gaze darting across the grainy image.

"Here." Artemis pointed at a small detail in the background of the murder scene, the corner of a red car barely visible behind a dumpster. It was only a partial view, but the vibrant hue seemed to scream for attention amidst the dark and gruesome setting. "Doesn't that car look familiar?"

"Maybe," Forester said hesitantly, furrowing his brow in concentration. "I'm not sure. Why? What's so special about it?"

"Look closer," Artemis urged him, her fingers steadying the edges of the laptop screen as if trying to will more information from the pixels. "The shape of the taillight, the curve of the bumper... It's the same car from the third video."

"The what?"

But Artemis was nodding, already moving the cursor to click on a separate video file.

As she did, a new image popped into view. This video was one of the earlier ones posted.

Forester stared as Artemis tapped her finger on a parking lot. There, far in the background, another red car.

"Shit. You remembered that?"

"Photographic memory, remember?"

"No. Mine's more like a goldfish memory."

"Funny. But look!" She pointed. "Same car as the other one. What if it's his?"

"Could be a coincidence. Not a very uncommon model."

"Yeah, but in that color? And see, look... the license plate." She strained her eyes. "It's somewhat visible, isn't it?"

"Okay, hold on," Forester said, zooming in on the image. As the digital noise cleared up, the outline of a license plate became faintly visible, its characters distorted by shadows. Artemis squinted, trying to make out the numbers before turning to Forester.

"Can you enhance this any further?" she asked, her voice tense with suppressed excitement.

"Let me try," Forester replied, fingers flying across the keyboard as he applied filters to the image. Slowly, the plate became more legible, revealing a partial sequence of numbers and letters.

"Four... Z... something... N," Artemis whispered, her heart pounding in her chest as she committed the characters to memory. "We might have something here, Forester."

"Damn," Forester muttered, his earlier frustration replaced by a newfound sense of determination. "I'll run this through our database, see if we can get a match."

"Good." Artemis straightened up, feeling the weight of their discovery settle on her shoulders.

This could very well be the break they were looking for.

CHAPTER 11

The darkness inside the car was oppressive, the silence punctuated only by the steady hum of the engine and the occasional flicker of a streetlight casting eerie shadows across the faces of Artemis, Forester, and Agent Wade. They sat in tense anticipation, their eyes trained on the inconspicuous mechanic's shop where the red car was registered.

Artemis fiddled with the hem of her shirt, her fingers trembling ever so slightly. Her heart pounded in her chest, each beat echoing through her ears like the ticking of a bomb about to detonate.

"Relax, Artemis," Forester murmured, his voice low, barely audible. The tall man's voice was steady as ever, as if they were simply out for a nighttime joyride rather than a potential confrontation with a serial killer. "We're just here for some information."

"Easy for you to say," she whispered back, her eyes darting between the mechanic's shop and the gun that rested on Agent Wade's lap.

Wade sat quietly by Forester, sitting in the driver's seat.

Artemis had never been comfortable around weapons and the proximity now only served to heighten her anxiety. Especially with what was at stake. Part of her wished Helen had come along, but another part of her was glad that her sister had returned home. They'd continue shopping for mansions in the morning.

At least, that was the plan.

"Here," Forester said, extending something back to her.

The dim glow of the dashboard lights cast eerie shadows across Artemis' face, her eyes darting between the house and the gun that Forester had just placed in her trembling hands. The cold metal felt heavy, foreign, like a weight she wasn't sure she could bear.

"Remember your training; you learned from the best," Forester said.

"You trained her, right?" Wade asked.

"Mhmm."

"Figures."

Artemis nodded, swallowing hard as she tightened her grip on the weapon. She had never been comfortable around guns, but she knew that her survival—and the success of their mission – might very well depend on her ability to use one.

"Are we sure this is the right place—the right car?" Her voice wavered slightly as she gestured with her free hand toward the mechanic shop, its neon sign flickering in the darkness.

Agent Wade wiggled his phone which he'd used to access the information they had gathered earlier. Artemis watched him intently.

"Yep; triple checked. Car is registered to the owner here," Wade confirmed, nodding as he looked up from his screen. "No doubt about it. Only make and model that matches the partial you found."

Normally, Wade didn't speak in such long sentences. She supposed tonight was a special occasion; they were hoping to catch a psycho.

"Okay," Artemis replied, trying to push away the doubts that still gnawed at her.

She focused, leveling her attentive, intelligent gaze on the structure across the street, watching the flickering light on the first floor, which glowed out and spilled like honey onto the street.

The machine shop was a sprawling, single-story structure with peeling paint and brightly lit windows. Its once-bright blue exterior had faded to a dull gray, like an aging bruise beneath the skin of the city. The air carried the tangy scent of engine oil and the persistent hum of machinery. To any casual observer, it appeared as though nothing unusual took place within its worn walls.

Artemis couldn't help but scrutinize the building, her gaze drawn to the shadows that seemed to shift in the back. Her intuition told her there was more than met the eye—something sinister lurking behind the veil of normalcy. Her breath hitched as she caught sight of two men standing outside the shop's entrance, their imposing figures radiating an air of menace.

"Those guards," she whispered, careful not to draw attention. "Seems strange to have guards at a machine shop."

"Rough part of town," Forester said, his brow furrowing. "But either way, we're going to have to find a way past them."

"Without causing a scene," Agent Wade added, his voice low and tense.

"Right." Artemis chewed on her lower lip, her mind whirring with possibilities. How were they going to bypass the guards without arousing suspicion? She glanced down at the gun in her hand and felt a shiver of apprehension ripple through her. Could she really use it if necessary?

She nodded, swallowing hard. Forester was right—she had come too far to let fear hold her back now. Taking a deep breath, she steeled herself for the challenge ahead.

"Maybe we can create a diversion," Forester suggested, his gaze locked on the guards. "Something to draw them away from their post."

"Like what?" Wade asked.

"Fire alarm?"

"You see one of those, hotshot?"

"Damn, Wade. What's got your panties in a bunch. Nookie from Dr. Bryant gone cold?"

"Dr. Bryant?" Artemis chimed in.

Wade looked away, pretending he hadn't heard her.

Artemis pictured the purple-haired coroner with the paste-on eyelashes. She'd always had a soft spot for Dr. Bryant.

And Dr. Bryant had a soft spot of a different variety for Wade.

A sudden flash of memory reminded Artemis of the last time she'd seen the two of them; Bryant had commented on Wade's chest muscles.

Now, however, Artemis' own chest was aching. She felt like a caged animal, trapped inside the car and desperate for a way out. And then, an idea struck her.

"I could do it," Artemis blurted out before she could stop herself. The two agents turned to look at her.

"Do what?" Forester asked, narrowing his eyes.

"Draw them out. I could pretend to be lost or looking for someone. It might be enough to get them away from the shop – at least long enough for you two to sneak in. I don't look like a threat."

"I find you threatening," Forester said.

"Er, thank you."

"Sure. But also, absolutely not." Forester's voice was firm, protective. "It's too dangerous, Artemis. We can't risk putting you in harm's way."

"I know this is risky, but I also know that we're running out of time. Those movies from the dark web keep playing in my mind." She shivered. "I wish I'd never seen them."

She could see the internal struggle playing out on Forester's face, his concern for her safety warring with their shared desire to bring the killer to justice. But this wasn't just about her anymore—it was about all the lives that hung in the balance, all the people who could be saved if they succeeded in finding the Prodigy or the dirextor.

Forester hesitated, his gaze flicking between her pleading face and the guards outside the shop.

Wade was the one who broke the stalemate. "Yeah. Good call. Just don't get too close."

"Hang on," Forester cut in. "Not a good call."

"Yes, it is," Wade insisted.

Artemis was already pushing out the door, though. Glad to be rid of the confines. Sometimes, sitting still was far worse than motion. She knew in chess that activity didn't always mean progress.

But stagnant positioning often meant an opponent was developing some strategy that would blindside you.

She needed to move.

As she slipped out the car door, the cold night air rushed in, bringing with it a sense of urgency and danger that set her nerves on edge.

"Good luck," Wade murmured, his eyes never leaving the guards.

"Thanks," she whispered.

She shut the door quietly, and strode across the street, moving over the sidewalk with surefooted steps, her figure illuminated briefly by the dim glow of a nearby streetlight before she vanished into the shadows.

The shadows seemed to cling to Artemis as she approached the guards. Her footsteps were muffled by the soft, damp earth beneath her, and she mentally rehearsed her plan one last time.

Granted, it wasn't really a plan.

More like the attempt at a plan.

"Hey!" she called out cheerfully, her voice wavering slightly despite her best efforts to keep it steady.

The two men looked at her.

It felt like they were twice as large up close, both of them wearing grease-stained overalls.

The man on the right looked like an advertisement for steroid overuse. He had a bald head, a thick neck, and a five o'clock shadow that could put a lumberjack to shame. His beady eyes flicked over her as though she were a piece of meat on display.

"What do you want?" he growled, his voice low and menacing.

"I'm looking for my friend," Artemis said, trying to sound innocent and helpless. "I think he might have come in here."

The second man, who was taller and leaner, snorted. "I'd be happy to help you, hon. I think I'm the fella you're lookin' for."

Artemis forced a smile despite the rising sense of unease in her chest.

The first man stepped forward, closing the distance between them. She could smell the sweat on his skin and the faint scent of cigarettes and alcohol on his breath.

"You shouldn't be out here alone," he said, his voice low and dangerous. "It ain't safe."

Artemis felt a jolt of fear shoot through her. Normally, she would never have invoked her brother's name...

Not for something like this.

But in this part of the city?

Her brother was not known for his subtlety and discretion. And for better or worse, the chances of them at least knowing Tommy's name were high.

"You guys know Tommy Blythe?" she said quickly.

The guards exchanged glances, their stony expressions giving way to suspicion. They shifted uneasily in their places.

"Who's asking?" One of them growled, narrowing his eyes at the seemingly innocuous young woman before him.

"His sister," Artemis replied smoothly, offering them a tentative smile. "We were supposed to meet here."

"Tommy's sister, huh?" The other guard scoffed, his lip curling in contempt.

"We know Tommy," the first man said, sneering.

It wasn't with any sort of fondness that he spoke the name.

"Oh?" she said.

"Yeah, we know Tommy well."

He took a step towards her again, and she took another step back.

"You can tell your brother that he owes us big time. That little weasel stole a bunch of cash from the craps table." He pointed a finger at her. "You here to bring our money back?"

She swallowed. "Er... umm..." She took another hesitant step back.

Artemis felt a cold shiver run down her spine, but she forced herself to maintain her composure. This was her chance—if she could just get these men angry enough, she might be able to draw them out and away from the shop.

"Sure," she said. "I've got the money. Just... you need to come with me."

"Your brother's a rat," the first guard snarled, stepping forward menacingly. "Rat runs in the blood. Don't it?"

Both men were now moving towards her. She saw the one with the bulging muscles tense.

His eyes flashed.

And then he lunged at her with a shout.

She yelped, already stumbling back and turning on her heel. Artemis broke into a dead sprint, back in the direction of the waiting car. As she fled, she felt a surge of gratitude for illegal steroids.

What they provided in bulk and vascularity, they diminished in speed and endurance.

Both men were coming after her, but she realized, after a few sprinting steps, that she would have to slow to allow them the hope of catching her.

She moved through the shadows, swiftly, occasionally shooting glances over her shoulder to track the guards' progress.

As she raced through the darkness, her pulse thundering, Artemis prayed that Forester would be ready to intervene—and soon.

Not because the goons behind her were closing the distance, but rather because they seemed to be lagging behind, and on the verge of giving up the chase.

Artemis had lost sight of the FBI vehicle. It wasn't where they'd parked initially.

She frowned, staring toward the empty shadows.

What the hell?

Where were they?

She heard a shout and glanced back to see one of the goons had pulled a switchblade, the weapon reflecting the moonlight menacingly.

Artemis ducked down a side alley, her gaze glancing one final time towards where the car should've been parked.

Why had they moved?

Perhaps they'd been worried they would be spotted when she came towards them.

But if so, where the hell were they now?

Her boots pounded against the concrete as she ran for her life. The sound of her pursuers echoed behind her, and she could feel their presence closing in. Adrenaline coursed through her veins as she pushed herself faster, desperately searching for an escape.

The alley seemed to stretch on forever, buildings rising up like jagged teeth on either side, trapping Artemis in a claustrophobic tunnel of shadows and fear. She glanced back to see that the goons were still following her, blocking any chance of escape.

They seemed to have caught a second wind now that they were running down the alley.

As if they knew something she didn't, which propelled their footsteps.

The thought sent a shiver down her spine, accompanying the chill night breeze.

She glanced ahead and froze.

With a sinking feeling in the pit of her stomach, Artemis realized that this was it—a dead end with no way out.

CHAPTER 12

Artemis' breath came in shallow gasps as she frantically searched for another option—an open window or door—but there was nothing but brick walls and locked doors around her. Panic clawed at her throat and sweat beaded on her forehead as she spun around to face the two thugs who had been chasing her down the alleyway.

They were both huge men wearing dark clothes and heavy boots. Both of them had menacing expressions on their faces as they stalked closer towards Artemis, their eyes glittering with malice in the moonlight.

The one with the switchblade gripped it tightly, his steroid-infused muscles bulging like strange barnacles.

She could hear her own breath coming in rapid pants.

"Hey there, girlie," snarled the steroid-user.

She didn't reply, her back pressing against the cold stone.

And then there was a reply from the mouth of the alley.

"Hey yourself," came the cavalier reply.

The two goons turned sharply, glancing back toward the tall, lanky figure standing in the mouth of the alley. Forester stepped forward, his tall frame casting a long shadow that seemed to swallow the guards in their tracks.

The two goons had turned sharply now, both of them hesitant, cautious. Their nonverbal cues had changed completely. Instead of cocksure, predatory, they were now hesitant, alarmed.

"Going somewhere?" Forester asked coolly, his voice echoing against the brick walls of the alley. The guards, momentarily stunned, exchanged uncertain glances before they refocused on the man standing between them and their prey.

"Who the hell are you?" the first guard barked, trying to mask his unease with bravado.

There were two of them and only one of Cameron, but the lupine confidence with which Forester stalked slowly towards them put them both ill at ease.

Plus, she realized, they were staring at the gun on his hip.

Forester tapped the weapon, his eyes hooded, dangerous.

She'd seen this look before, and it always made her skin crawl.

Sometimes, it was as if her boyfriend vanished, and something darker swallowed him. She could see it in the eyes, and it came out whenever she was threatened, as if, in a deeply unsettling way, her well-being was Forester's anchor to sanity.

But now, she was cornered, and Cameron was rolling his shoulders, still stepping forward.

"Don't mind this old thing," Cameron muttered, tapping his gun.

The two goons shifted nervously.

But then, Cameron pulled the weapon from his pocket, and with practiced motions jettisoned the live round, caught it, and then pulled the magazine out, slipping it into his pocket.

"See?" he said, "Empty."

He holstered the gun again.

The two goons shared a confused look, but glanced back at Cameron, scowling at him.

Mr. Steroids stepped forward now, knife clutched tightly, chin wagging.

"What the hell you think you're doing here? I don't recognize you. You with this bitch?" He jammed a finger over his shoulder towards where Artemis remained pressed against the wall.

And only then, her back against cold stone, did she realize she still had the gun Forester had given her. She could feel it cold against her back where she'd tucked it in the back of her waistband.

She reached for it, hesitantly.

But Forester noticed the movement and gave a small little shake of his head.

Not in warning, nor really out of any sort of concern. In a way, he almost looked childish, like a toddler pleading for five more minutes before bedtime.

He seemed worried she would take his fun.

She felt silly now. They'd moved the car so they could ambush the goons, but all along, they'd known she was armed.

They must've seen the guards weren't.

She'd completely forgotten about the gun, as if she'd simply wanted to forget about it, her mind choosing to ignore the discomfort.

But now, Forester was within a couple steps of the two goons.

The one with the knife was holding his weapon tightly, his teeth gritted.

"There's two of us, big guy," snapped Steroids.

"Mhmm. Wish there were more."

Again, the goons exchanged an uncomfortable glance. The one with the knife and the muscles moved forward hesitantly, knife brandished in front of him.

Forester didn't react at first.

"Come on, pretty boy," sneered one of the thugs, lunging for Cameron.

Forester seemed unfazed. As he dodged the thug's clumsy attempts to grab him, he seemed perfectly in control. He moved with a fluidity and precision that was almost hypnotic to watch.

Artemis couldn't help but admire his composure. It was clear that he wasn't even remotely concerned about the two men trying to accost him.

Both men were now moving forward, cautious at first, but with more irritation—Artemis realized Cameron was leading them away from her.

Forester's eyes sparkled mischievously as he playfully slapped away the thugs' hands, his movements fluid and graceful like a dancer. The frustrated scowls on their faces only seemed to amuse him more, and he chuckled lightly under his breath—but the lupine quality to his gaze never disappeared. As Artemis watched, she couldn't help but marvel at the way he effortlessly toyed with them, as though they were nothing more than pesky flies buzzing about his head.

"Come on, is that really the best you've got?" Forester taunted, still dodging their increasingly desperate attempts to grab hold of him.

"Shut up!" growled the first thug, his heavily muscled frame quivering with barely contained rage. Years of steroid use had left him with bulging arms and a barrel chest, which only served to make his frustration all the more palpable. His companion, leaner and less imposing, looked nervously between Forester and his partner, as if unsure of how to proceed in the face of such unexpected resistance.

The veins on the heavily muscled thug's forehead bulged like angry earthworms, his frustration evident in the way he clenched his fists at his sides, the knife in his right hand trembling.

The thug lunged forward in an attempt to stab Forester. Time seemed to slow down, every detail of the attack etching itself into Artemis' mind—the desperate gleam in the thug's eyes, the flex of his muscles as he struck, the cold steel of the knife slicing through the air.

But Forester was a step ahead. With lightning-fast reflexes, he caught the thug's wrist, twisting it just enough to send the knife clattering onto the grimy pavement. The thug gaped in disbelief, his grip on the weapon gone.

"Oops," Forester teased, bending down to pick up the knife. He twirled it between his fingers like a party trick before extending it hilt-first toward the disarmed attacker. "Here you go. Try again."

"Wh-what the hell?" stammered the thug, taking the knife back with a mix of astonishment and anger.

The disbelief etched on the thug's face quickly morphed into seething frustration as he lunged at Forester again, knife raised. Artemis held her breath.

Cameron sidestepped the attack and effortlessly relieved the thug of his weapon once more. The blade spun in the air before landing perfectly in Forester's outstretched hand, eliciting a growl from the furious attacker.

"Now, now," Forester said. "Let's give your friend a turn, shall we?"

He extended the knife towards the second, thinner man.

But this fellow was staring at Cameron as if he'd seen a ghost. "N-no, thank you," he said.

Cameron flashed his wolfish smile. "Thank you? We're being polite now, aren't we? I thought you two had just called my girlfriend a bitch?"

Both men stared at Cameron, glanced back at Artemis, and then the horror could be seen etched across their faces.

"W-we didn't.... didn't know!"

Suddenly, Steroids turned sharply and tried to sprint towards Artemis, clearly realizing she was his best bet at beating Cameron.

But again, Forester anticipated the move.

He lunged, catching the man by the collar and dragging him back.

"That was a mistake," Cameron growled. The mischief was gone from his eyes—all that remained was feral.

The thug's eyes bulged in shock as he felt the grip of Forester's iron-clad fingers. He tried to wriggle free, but it was no use.

Then, as if bored of an activity, Cameron ended it.

He proceeded to deliver two vicious blows, one to the thug's stomach and another to his jaw.

The man collapsed to the ground, unconscious.

The second man held out hands in protest. "Wait! Don't!"

But he was caught by an uppercut from the ex-fighter's fist. His head snapped back, and he clattered against the wall, toppling to the ground in a heap.

Forester stepped over them both, the rage on his face slowly subsiding as he turned back towards Artemis.

"Are you alright?"

Artemis nodded weakly. "Yes," she said softly, her heart still racing from the adrenaline rush that had coursed through her body during the altercation.

Cameron extended his scarred hand towards her. "Let's get out of here," he said with a nod of his head towards their attackers' prone forms. "Before they wake up."

The piercing shriek of an engine jolted Artemis from the haze of adrenaline that still pulsed through her veins. She whipped around, her heart pounding as she saw a red car tearing out of the shadowy recesses of the mechanic shop's garage. Her eyes widened, and her breath hitched in her throat; they were running out of time.

"Forester, the car!" she cried out, her voice desperate.

"Shit!" he muttered under his breath, immediately turning towards the sound.

They sprinted back towards the mouth of the alley.

With a screech of tires, a second car appeared right in front of them.

"Get in, get in!" Agent Wade called out, his eyes flicking between the unconscious guards and the fleeing red car.

Artemis threw herself into the backseat, the cold leather chilling her skin as she scrambled to secure her seatbelt. Her heart pounded in her throat. As Forester settled into the front passenger seat, he caught her eye in the rearview mirror—a brief, silent exchange that communicated more than words ever could.

"Go!" he barked, his voice sharp and urgent.

"Damn it," Wade muttered, flooring the gas pedal as their car lurched forward. Artemis gripped the door handle tightly, knuckles turning white as they tore through the night, the red taillights of their quarry glowing like embers in the darkness.

"He's fast!" Forester warned.

Wade just grunted, eyes fixated on the road as they raced, under the cover of night, in pursuit of a suspected serial killer.

CHAPTER 13

The car's engine roared as they sped after their target, weaving through the streets with reckless abandon. Artemis could feel the raw power beneath her feet where she sat in the back as Wade urged the vehicle forward. Her gaze remained fixed on the red car, its taillights burning bright like the eyes of a demon in the night.

The tension in the car was palpable, like a live wire threatening to snap at any moment. Artemis' heart pounded in her chest as she gripped the door handle tightly, knuckles white from the strain. The sound of the engine and the tires screeching against the pavement filled her ears, drowning out everything else.

"Keep up," Cameron ordered, his voice cold and controlled. "We can't afford to lose him."

Agent Wade nodded, his eyes never leaving the road ahead. His hands moved with practiced precision, guiding the car through the winding streets and narrow alleys. There was an artistry to his driving that couldn't be denied; every turn was calculated, each maneuver executed with skill.

"Get me closer," Cameron said, his voice tense but firm. "I need a clean shot at the tires."

Artemis watched as they closed in on the red car, her anxiety mounting with each passing second. She tried to calm herself by focusing on her breathing, just as she'd been taught. Inhale for four counts, hold for four, exhale for four. The familiar rhythm helped to steady her nerves, even as her thoughts raced with the implications of what would happen if they failed to apprehend the suspect.

"Almost there," Wade said, his voice steady despite the adrenaline coursing through his veins. "Just hang on."

Cameron nodded, his gaze locked on the fleeing vehicle. He raised his gun, preparing to fire once they were within range.

"Go for the tires!" Wade shouted over the roar of the engine.

Without hesitation, Cameron gripped his gun tightly and leaned out of the window, the wind whipping through his usually disheveled hair as he took aim. Artemis held her breath, her heart pounding in her chest as she watched him. This was it – their one chance to bring the suspect to justice.

"Come on, come on," Cameron muttered under his breath, his eyes narrowing as he tried to line up his shot.

"Damn it!" Cameron cursed as he fired two shots at the fleeing vehicle, the sound deafening in the confined space of the car. Artemis flinched, her hands instinctively covering her ears as she fought to stay focused.

Cameron's shots whizzed past the swerving red car, clipping the bumper but missing the tires.

The red car swerved to the left, avoiding the passenger side now.

Its door scraped against the concrete barrier, sending out a flurry of sparks.

"No shot!" Cameron yelled. He was practically sitting in the window now but had to duck as they moved through a tight tunnel that dipped under a railroad.

"He's faster!" Wade shouted, gritting his teeth.

Artemis' mind whirred. She pieced together the eventualities. The scene played out in her mind like a choreographed dance.

Forester was on the right side of the car.

Wade was left but driving—he couldn't shoot.

Ahead, the fleeing car had realized the angles and was now driving on the left side of the road. Forester didn't have an angle to shoot at it unless he blasted through their own windshield.

Which meant it was down to her.

Forester was already unbuckling, suggesting he wanted to clamber into the backseat, but Artemis knew it would be too late.

Wade was right, the red car had hit another gear and was picking up speed.

Someone had done work to the engine—it was far faster than the simple chassis might have suggested.

She steadied her nerves, gripping the gun she'd been provided.

The wind whipped Artemis' face, stinging her eyes and tugging at her hair as she took a deep breath, steadying herself for the crucial shot. She could feel her heart pounding, heavy and insistent against her ribcage, a throbbing reminder of the stakes at hand.

She aimed out the window for the back tire. She forced herself to recount her training—the brief instances where Cameron had walked her through the process of shooting at a moving target.

She took a deep breath, held it, and then released it slowly. She could feel the tension in her shoulders dissipating as she exhaled.

Time seemed to slow as she steadied her breathing and lined up her shot.

Her finger wrapped around the trigger.

The red car was nearly too far now, still picking up pace; at any moment, it might veer onto a side street, and she'd lose line-of-sight. Its tires bounced over potholes as it sped ahead of them. The engine roared in her ears as she aligned the sights of her gun with the back tire.

There was no more time for hesitation.

Artemis took one last deep breath and fired off two shots in rapid succession, aiming for the back tire of the red car.

The first shot missed, but the second connected directly with the tire sending a shower of sparks flying as the rubber exploded, dropping the metal rim to the asphalt in a cacophony of metallic screaming.

The car drifted violently from side to side.

Forester shouted in triumph.

As the red car swerved out of control, Artemis allowed herself a small gasp, releasing pent-up breath. She dropped the gun in the seat next to her.

Ahead, the red car spun out, striking the concrete barrier.

It crashed in a shower of glass and metal, sending shards flying everywhere. The engine block buckled and the car came to a stop, smoke rising from its hood.

The force of the impact shook the air around them, and Artemis felt her heart sink as she took in the scene before her.

The red car was totaled, its frame crumpled and broken beyond recognition. The windshield had shattered into thousands of pieces that glinted like diamonds against the backdrop of dusk.

In the eerie silence that followed, Forester and Wade jumped out of their car with guns drawn.

"FBI!" they shouted. "Hands! Show us your hands!"

Artemis watched from the car. She could hear the sound of her own breathing, the only thing breaking the silence that had settled over the scene.

Seconds ticked by like hours as the agents waited for a response. Finally, the driver's door of the red car opened slowly, and a man stumbled out, his hands raised in surrender.

He was squat and muscled, with short black hair and a scruffy beard. His clothes were torn and stained with blood, and he looked dazed, as if unsure of where he was or what had just happened.

Forester and Wade approached him cautiously, their guns at the ready.

"Get down on the ground!" Forester ordered, his voice hard and unyielding.

The suspect complied, dropping to his knees with his hands still raised above his head.

"Please," he said, his voice shaking. "Don't shoot!"

Forester and Wade moved in, handcuffing him and patting him down for weapons.

Artemis watched as they led him back to their car, her mind still reeling from the intensity of the chase. She could feel her pulse racing, her body still trembling with adrenaline.

As the man was pushed towards her, he was shaking his head, gasping. "Hang on—just... just hang on! This is all a big misunderstanding."

She stared at the figure. He was shaking his head side to side, trying to protest as the agents tugged him toward the car.

She didn't recognize him at first. He was squat, compact. A muscled build but with more flab than Agent Wade. His hair was unkempt, but his beard was neatly trimmed and oiled.

It took her a few seconds, staring at him, for recognition to slowly dawn.

She stared.

And then muttered, "Oh shit."

Agent Wade seemed to be realizing the same thing at the same time. he was nudging Cameron, leaning in to whisper something.

Cameron's eyes told the story.

Even as he held the cuffed man, his eyes widened like saucers.

"Shit, really?" she heard Cameron say through the open window.

Artemis didn't know the man personally, but she'd seen him in news articles.

His father was the head of the Seattle mob, after all.

They had just arrested mob royalty.

She cycled through her mind, trying to recollect the articles she'd read.

Rico Santino.

Rico Santino had a mean reputation, but it wasn't anything compared to his father's.

Miles Santino ran half the criminal enterprises in the city. Miles was the boss, and everyone knew it.

What would he do when he found out the FBI had his son?

"Shit," Wade was saying, clearly thinking along similar lines.

Artemis just sat in the backseat, staring as Rico was pushed towards the car.

On an expose piece she'd once read, seven years and two months ago, she'd learned that fifty percent of the murders in Seattle could be traced back to Miles' dealings.

"Shit," Wade repeated, shaking his head as he opened the back door and shoved Rico in.

Forester looked more amused than concerned. "Mind if I get a selfie?" he asked.

Rico just stared at him.

Artemis tried to look small, glancing out the window.

Forester opened her door, though, gesturing for her to move to the front seat, as he slid in the back. Whether this was to protect her, or because he wanted another shot at the selfie wasn't apparent at first.

Rico was muttering under his breath, a series of threats that made Artemis' blood chill.

More than once, he said the phrase father.

But now... Artemis wondered if they'd caught the serial killer. Was he the dirextor? Had he been using the brazenness of his father's connections to get away with indiscriminate murder?

She shivered as she settled in the front seat, glancing in the rearview mirror.

Rico's eyes were as cold as ice.

He was still stammering, protesting, but his demeanor didn't match his supplicant tone.

He was a shark.

Sitting next to a wolf.

Artemis felt as if she were trapped in a predatory menagerie.

"So," Forester said conversationally, "We got a couple questions for ya, bud. Listen close."

CHAPTER 14

The police car screeched to a halt in front of the precinct. Artemis' heart pounded as she looked out the window, taking in the scene before her. Forester killed the engine, and they sat for a moment in silence.

"Alright," he said finally, "let's get this show on the road."

Artemis opened her door, feeling the cool night air rush in. She followed Forester and Wade out of the car, her eyes darting around the chaotic scene that unfolded outside the station. Forester guided Rico Santino ahead of himself, pushing the man along. Police vehicles were everywhere, their lights flashing like the finale of a fireworks display. Officers swarmed around, their weapons drawn, preparing for something intense. Even a SWAT team was present, their black uniforms contrasting with the red and blue strobes.

"Wow," muttered Wade, his voice tense. "What did we walk into?"

Forester glanced at him, then at Artemis. "We'll find out soon enough," he said, his tattooed neck tensing as he spoke. He gave Rico another little push, and the mobster's son cursed as he stumbled forward.

"Hey, you!" an armed officer called out as he approached them. "Get that suspect inside!"

As they made their way toward the entrance, Artemis tried to focus on keeping her composure. She felt a knot growing in her stomach, tightening with each step they took.

Clearly, all the stops had been pulled out for the arrival of mob royalty.

"Stay close," Forester instructed her as they reached the stairs leading up to the precinct.

"Got it," Artemis whispered, her voice barely audible above the din of activity.

Her mind raced as they climbed the steps, the knot in her stomach pulling tighter. This was far more than she had bargained for when she agreed to help Forester and Wade apprehend Rico.

Artemis gazed around, her eyes wide as she took in the extent of the police presence. She had known that Rico Santino was a high-profile suspect, but this was beyond anything she had imagined. As the son of the Seattle godfather, Rico's capture was sure to send shockwaves through the city's criminal underworld, and Artemis couldn't help but wonder how many of these officers were here just for him.

"Quite the welcoming committee you've got out here," Rico commented, his voice dripping with sarcasm as he moved down the adjoining hall past the sergeant's desk. "You guys must really be desperate to pin something on me."

"Save it for inside," Wade said, guiding Rico by the arm a few steps forward.

"Easy there, cowboy," Rico muttered, grinning all the while.

Artemis followed closely behind, trying her best to blend into the background and avoid the attention of the news crews that had assembled outside the precinct, their cameras flashing through the windows.

"Hey! Where's my lawyer?" Rico demanded loudly, drawing the attention of several nearby officers, who shot him dirty looks. "I got rights, you know."

"Your lawyer will be here shortly," Wade responded curtly. "Until then, sit down and shut up."

They ushered Rico into one of the interrogation rooms, its cold, sterile environment offering no comfort to those it housed. A single metal table and two chairs were bolted to the floor in the center of the room, while a harsh fluorescent light buzzed overhead. Artemis couldn't help but shudder at the sight, imagining herself in the same position as Rico – alone, facing judgment.

"Take a seat," Forester ordered, pushing Rico down into one of the chairs.

Artemis stood by the door, observing the interaction from a distance. Rico looked around the room, his smirk temporarily replaced by a hint of apprehension. It seemed, for a moment, that the gravity of his situation had finally sunk in.

"Nice place you've got here," he quipped, trying to regain his composure. "Really makes a guy feel at home."

"Cut the crap, Rico," Wade snapped.

Artemis retreated to the far corner of the room, her simple attire blending seamlessly with the drab walls. From here, she could observe Rico Santino's interrogation without drawing attention to herself. She watched as Forester and Wade circled their prey, their gazes unwavering.

"Rico," Forester began, his voice a blend of sternness and feigned friendliness. "We found this red car abandoned not far from the last murder scene." He tossed a photograph onto the table, the image showing a sleek crimson vehicle parked in a dark alleyway. "Now, isn't that your car?"

"Is it registered to me?" Rico said smugly.

It wasn't. The car was registered to one Ralph Swanson, that's why they didn't realize who they were following until they pulled Rico from the car. But when Wade had followed up on the registration, it became clear that there was no such person. It would have been clever to register the car under a patsy's name, but Artemis could already tell that cleverness only mattered to Rico if he could use it to embarrass others or aggrandize himself.

Forester grinned right back at the mobster. "I kinda assumed you just misspelled your name there, friend. Y'know, since Ralph doesn't exist. Either way, you had the car, drove the car, and crashed the car, so unless you want to miraculously call in this 'Ralph', we're just going to add the forged registration to your charges and call it good, alright?"

Rico rolled his eyes and chuckled. "Ooo, spooky. What do you want, a cookie? Yeah, it's my car. Sure is a beauty, ain't it?" His eyes flicked over the photo for only a moment before returning to meet Forester's gaze. "But that doesn't mean I know anything about these murders."

"Really?" Wade interjected, holding up a tablet. He tapped the screen, and a grainy video clip played. "Looks like your plates, no?"

"Hey, lots of people drive red cars," Rico countered dismissively, crossing his arms over his chest. "How do you know it's me? I only see a couple of letters and shit."

"It's your car. Your plates are unique for your make and model." Forester winked. "You're a special little boy, aren't you?"

Rico shrugged. "I don't know where that was, man. I go a lot of places."

"Yeah? How about two murder scenes? Just so happened to be at both during the commission of the crime?"

Forester put a second photo on the table from the later video they'd found on the dark web.

Rico stared from one photo to the other.

"Start talking, Rico," Forester demanded, leaning in closer.

Rico's fingers drummed nervously on the table, his eyes darting between Forester and Wade. He licked his lips, a bead of sweat trickling down his temple.

"Look," he began, attempting a smirk, "I don't know anything about any murders, okay? I just borrowed that car from a friend. No idea it was involved in any... shady business."

"Really?" Forester pressed, his piercing gaze never leaving Rico. "And what friend would that be?"

"Uh, you know..." Rico hesitated, the cockiness in his voice fading. "A guy named Tony. Yeah, Tony."

Wade leaned in, her eyes narrowed. "So you expect us to believe that your 'friend' Tony handed you the keys to a car connected to multiple gruesome murders, and you had no idea?"

"Hey," Rico protested, feigning offense. "I can't keep tabs on everything my friends do. I just needed a ride, alright?"

Artemis watched from her corner, her dual-colored eyes flicking between the three figures. Her mind raced as she tried to discern whether Rico's story held any truth or if it was merely a desperate attempt to evade responsibility.

"Rico," Forester said, leaning back in his chair. "Do you really think we're going to buy that? The car has been registered to your alias for like sixteen years. Try again."

"Tony borrowed the car!" Rico said. "It was *basically* his for like two years."

"Tony borrowed the car for two years?"

"That's right."

"And who's this Tony fellow?"

"Look, I didn't ask questions," Rico insisted, his voice wavering. "He said he needed to use the car for a few days, so he did. What happened before or after is not on me."

"That's not what you said a few seconds ago. Your story changing, huh Rico?"

"I'm stressed, man. Chill."

"Convenient," Wade remarked with a sardonic smile. "The son of the Seattle Godfather just happens to loan a car to a friend, which also happens to be connected to two murders. But of course, you knew nothing about it."

Artemis could see the tension building in Rico's shoulders, his façade crumbling with each passing moment. She wondered if he would break.

"Enough!" Rico snapped, slamming his hands on the table. "I'm telling you, I don't know anything! I just borrowed the damn car!"

"Then maybe it's time we have a chat with this Tony," Forester suggested.

"Go ahead," Rico spat, his eyes blazing with defiance. "But you won't find anything on me."

"Got a name? An address?"

"No," Rico said, sullenly, crossing his arms.

Artemis observed his body language. Defensive. Frightened. All bluster, no bite. Not really.

The air in the room seemed to constrict, thick with tension and unspoken words. The two agents stared at Rico, their gazes sharp as daggers. Artemis, observing from the corner, felt a chill run down her spine.

"Alright, Rico," Forester began, his voice steady and cold. "Let's talk about your father. Tell us more about your relationship with him."

Rico shifted uncomfortably in his chair, beads of sweat forming on his brow. "What's there to say? He's my father. We're not close, but we're not enemies either."

"Interesting," Wade interjected, his eyes narrowing. "Considering your father's reputation, it seems odd that you'd just loan out a car without knowing what it would be used for. Seems like a liability when your name is on the registration, doesn't it?"

"Maybe I don't ask questions I don't want the answers to."

"Or maybe you know more than you're admitting. Tony got a last name?"

Artemis watched as Rico clenched his fists, his knuckles turning white. "Wait, hang on! Yeah. Yeah, I think I remember him a bit better now."

"Tony who?" Wade said, firmly.

"Tony Caruso," Rico reluctantly replied, averting his gaze.

"Where can we find this Tony Caruso?"

"Man, I don't know!" Rico practically shouted, slamming his hands on the table. "He doesn't tell me everything. He's just... he's just an associate!"

"An associate who borrows your car during high-profile murders," Wade pointed out dryly.

"Fine, I'll try to remember where he might be," Rico said, "but I need some assurances."

"What type of assurances?" Wade countered.

"Here's your assurance," Forester said quietly, "We won't tell your old man that you ratted someone out, how about that?"

Artemis watched closely now. She called out, "He's making the name up."

All three sets of eyes turned towards her.

"Come again?" Forester said.

She shook her head. "There's no Tony. He's making him up."

She hadn't been a hundred percent sure at first, but now, judging by Rico's reaction, she realized she was right. It was in his tone, his brash attitude.

It had taken a moment for her to peg him.

What he was.

A spoiled child. Of course, he was a grown man but in arrested development. She knew people—knew nonverbals.

And Rico was petulant. Everything about him screamed my-daddy-can-beat-up-your-daddy.

He was now glaring at her, fury in his gaze. But she kept calm, and repeated, "There's no one named Tony."

She looked at him, stepping from the light and watching him. "I know something about having a notorious father."

"Oh yeah, what the hell did your daddy do?"

"Have you ever heard of the Ghost Killer?" she said.

Wade and Forester were watching her cautiously now.

But she was in the zone.

It was how she often felt in moments like these; a slow buildup of information and then a sudden burst of insight.

It was like analysis before a competition.

She'd won her first blitz match after sacrificing her rooks. And now she wanted to make a similar trade: information for information.

She knew men like this. Street cred mattered to them. But they also had a severe distrust of law enforcement. Their whole lives, they'd feasted on stories about the injustice various members of their families may or may not have actually experienced at the hands of the boys in blue.

Cops were the enemy. Feds doubly so.

Now, Rico was eying her. "Yeah—heard. Was in the news some time. So what?"

"He's my father," she said simply.

Of course, the *real* Ghost Killer hadn't been her father, but Otto Blythe had been convicted of the murders—which, as far as Rico was concerned, was all that mattered.

He frowned at her. "Oh, shit—yeah, I think I recognize you. Atticus or something, right? Some stupid-ass name."

She didn't take the bait. "You're local? Yeah? Keep an ear to the ground?"

"So what? You think Imma just spill my guts cuz your daddy happens to be some sicko?"

"No," she said softly. "I was simply making a point. You think your father will protect you, yes?"

He just glared at her.

"But what about behind bars," she said quietly. She was prodding, needling, figuring out the weaknesses, figuring out where his defenses were, and also where she might exploit them.

It was all a dance.

But at her words, he started frowning. "We got people behind bars," he snapped. "You can't scare me, bitch."

"Mhmm. My father is behind bars," she said quietly.

"I thought your old man escaped."

"No," she lied. "He turned himself in. He missed it, you know. They treat him like a king in there. He killed seven women, eight some say."

"Why the hell are you telling me this?"

"They found some of the dead girls in his bed, sleeping with him," she continued softly. "He strangled some of them. Others... You don't even want to know."

Rico was now staring at her, hanging onto her every word.

As she'd thought, he wasn't a trigger man. He wasn't some tough guy.

He was all posture, all fear.

She continued, "My dad has friends behind bars. I wonder," she said slowly, glancing at Forester, "could we get a judge to send Rico here to the same prison as my father? Maybe they could be cellmates."

"We can definitely assign him to a specific cell," Forester said immediately.

Wade just frowned, his lips pursed.

Normally, Artemis might have felt a certain way about taking this tack, but where Rico was concerned, she didn't have a problem with a bluff.

Rico was sweating profusely now. "You can't do that," he muttered. "I got connections."

"Oh," Artemis said, "I'm sure you do." She turned her head to Forester. "Can you make that happen?"

Forester nodded. "Easily."

Rico looked like he was about to pass out. His connections only worked in certain circles. There was a hierarchy in prisons. People had their cliques, their groups. But then there were the ones that were best avoided.

The men considered too dangerous to interact with or bribe—too unhinged.

Serial killers often fell into this latter category.

She could see it in his eyes now as he played out the scenario in his imagination. The idea of being cooped in the same cell as a serial killer.

"What do you want from me?" he said hoarsely.

"Why was your car at both crime scenes," she replied quietly.

"I told you."

"You lied."

"Shit," he said. "Look... Look, dammit. I really did let a guy borrow it. Two weeks."

"Not good enough," Artemis replied.

"I swear! I swear. I can prove it!" He exclaimed. "Hell—I got it on my phone. Bastard didn't return the car at first, so I had to threaten the prick. It's all on my phone."

Forester pulled out the confiscated phone from a gray plastic tupperware under the table. He placed it on the metal surface and turned the device so it was facing Rico.

"Password?" Forester said.

Rico hesitated, his hands still cuffed. Clearly still nervous.

But Artemis' gaze was unwavering. She didn't look away, and he let out a faint breath, scowling as he shook his head and hastily entered his passcode.

"The messages would've been from a while ago," Forester informed Wade.

Desmond was already cycling through the phone.

Artemis watched with mounting anticipation as Desmond's fingers flew across the keypad.

"Two weeks back," Wade said. He turned the phone for the others to see.

Artemis and Forester both leaned in, close. His breath was warm against her cheek, but her eyes fixated on the screen, reading the texts.

In them, Rico was clearly pissed. Where the hell is my car, man?

The other man's replies were evasive. Nothing that could be used as evidence.

But at least it was proof.

Rico had either given the car to someone or loaned it out.

And when he'd found out it wasn't returned, he'd threatened the man.

Artemis glanced at Rico, who was still looking sullen.

"Looks like you're vindicated," she said.

Rico's expression shifted. He was suspicious. "So what now? You just gonna let me go?"

"Depends," Forester cut in. "You gonna tell us who this number belongs too?"

"Y'all can't trace that shit or something?"

"We will. But you can give us a head start."

"Fine!" Rico said, irritated. "His name is Lemon."

"Lemon?"

"Not his real name. Like Lenny or something, but they call him Lemon. Sour prick. Real creep."

"How's he a creep?" Artemis said quickly.

Rico hesitated as if debating whether to divulge more information. But the thought of being sent to the same prison as a serial killer must have weighed heavily on his mind because he eventually relented. "He's just... off. You know? Like, he doesn't have any friends, doesn't talk to anyone. Just sits by himself and stares at people. And he always smells weird. Like he doesn't shower or something."

Artemis frowned, a feeling of unease settling in her stomach. "Can you give us an address?"

Rico nodded, rattling off an address on the outskirts of town. "But he might not be there. He moves around a lot. I only know that because I had to go pick up my car from him."

Rico slumped back in his chair, looking defeated. Artemis felt a flicker of sympathy for him, but it was quickly snuffed out by the knowledge of the crimes he had been involved in.

Wade leaned across the table and began speaking to Rico again, but Artemis' focus was distracted by something in Cameron's hand.

He had pulled up the address provided by Rico.

And on the screen, on his phone, there was a face that seemed to be staring out at them.

Pale, wide eyes. Hair slicked to the side over oily skin. Bright, red hair. His forehead was large—and in a way, he almost looked like a clown due to his pale, rosy skin.

Artemis frowned at the image. His eyes were too large, bulging like a toad's as it stared out at them.

She felt a flicker of unease.

Forester was swiping through the phone. "Small town crook," he said. "Nothing much on his sheet. He..."

"What?" Artemis said as Cameron trailed off.

He turned the phone so she could see clearly.

"Film school," Cameron said. "Kicked out of film school for making a pass at a female teacher."

Forester was already pushing to his feet. "Maybe we better pay Lemon a little visit."

CHAPTER 15

At nearly two in the morning, dirextor's car crept into his driveway like a shadow, the moon casting an eerie glow on the deserted street. The tires rolled silently over the gravel, coming to a gentle stop just before the garage door. The darkness seemed to envelop the vehicle as if nature itself conspired to keep its secrets.

"Almost there," he whispered, his breath fogging up the window.

The silence was shattered by a sudden thud from the trunk of the car. It was followed by muffled kicking sounds, desperate and frantic. Passion. He could practically taste the vitality. He could use that, *would* use it. Despite the concession in his username's spelling, dirextor was a director. No. Not just any director. *The* director. His heart raced, adrenaline pumping through his veins. He couldn't help but let out a small chuckle.

"Feisty one, aren't you?" he muttered under his breath, his eyes narrowed with anticipation.

He listened carefully to the erratic rhythm of the pounding from the trunk, each kick making him more eager for what was to come. He imagined the woman's fear, her eyes wide with terror.

To best the Prodigy, this impetuous upstart, he'd have to bring his 'A' game. Time to see just how exceptional she truly was.

The director's fingers drummed the steering wheel, resonating with the muffled thumps coming from the trunk of his car. He glanced around the darkened neighborhood, a predatory smirk playing upon his lips. The streetlights cast eerie shadows across the pavement, but there were no witnesses to his late-night activities. No one who could interrupt his work of art—his best one yet.

"Perfect," he whispered, his anticipation building like a raging storm.

He stepped out of the car, his shoes crunching on the gravel driveway. As he walked towards the trunk, the woman's frantic movements continued unabated. He could almost feel her desperation in the air, fueling his perverse excitement.

"Quiet now," he murmured, more to himself than to her. "Wouldn't want to spoil the fun too soon."

His fingers brushed against the cold metal latch, and he hesitated for just a moment before flinging the trunk open. His eyes locked onto the bound woman within, her eyes wide and fearful as they bore into his.

"Ah, there you are," the director said, his voice dripping with cruel satisfaction. "You're even more beautiful up close."

She was bound and gagged, her blonde hair shifting under her, spreading out like seaweed floating on water.

As he pulled her from the tight confines of the trunk, she struggled against his grip, her legs kicking wildly in an attempt to find freedom. But her efforts were futile; her captor was far stronger than she was.

Her gag slipped as she bucked, and she tried to scream, but he cupped her mouth.

She bit at his finger, but he only laughed, pulling his hand away as her teeth clicked together on empty air. He returned the attempt with a firm swat on the nose like disciplining an animal. "Now, now, don't be cruel."

"Please," she begged, tears streaming down her face. "I don't know what you want, but I'll do anything. Just let me go!"

"Anything?" The director raised an eyebrow, feigning interest. "What a tempting offer. But I'm afraid I only want one thing from you, and it's not something you can simply give."

He could feel her tremble beneath his grasp, the terror in her eyes a drug that sent a thrill up his spine. He knew he had complete control over her, and that thought alone was enough to send him spiraling into a dark abyss of sadistic pleasure.

"Let's get started, shall we?"

"Please, don't do this," she whimpered, her voice barely audible through the gag. Desperation fueled her resolve as she gathered all her strength and managed to wrench her arm free from the director's grasp.

"Damn you!" he hissed, momentarily caught off guard by her sudden defiance.

Seizing the opportunity, she stumbled forward, heart pounding and legs weak, attempting to put distance between herself and the monster that had ensnared her. Her uneven breaths were ragged and strained as her feet slipped on the dew-slicked grass.

"Stop! Stop, or I'll make it worse!" the director barked, but she pushed herself onward, driven by an overwhelming desire to survive.

But she was in no condition to flee. He lunged in and snagged her hair.

He dragged her forcefully towards the cellar door, the dark entrance looming like a gaping maw ready to swallow her whole.

The cellar door creaked open, revealing a poorly lit room filled with dusty shelves and cobwebs. The director shoved her inside, the force of his push causing her to trip over a stack of old boxes. She landed hard on the cold concrete floor, the impact sending shockwaves through her body.

"Get up," the director demanded, his voice echoing in the confined space. Her limbs trembled as she tried to stand, only for him to grab her arm in a bruising grip, dragging her further into the basement.

"Sit down," he ordered, shoving her towards an old wooden chair in the center of the room. Its legs scraped against the ground, making her wince at the sound.

"Please, what do you want from me?" she asked once more, desperation seeping into every word. He ignored her pleas, pushing her down onto the seat with enough force that it left her breathless.

"Quiet," he hissed, pulling out a length of coarse rope from one of the cluttered shelves. As he tied her wrists together behind the chair, he knew she would feel the fibers biting into her skin.

"Perfect," he muttered under his breath, stepping back to admire his handiwork.

The director reached onto a wooden shelf by the door, producing a small camcorder. He set it on a tripod a few feet away from her, adjusting its angle until it captured her terrified face perfectly in the frame.

"Smile for the camera," he taunted, flicking it on. The red recording light blinked menacingly, the lens focused like a hunter's scope.

"Wh-what do you want?" she stuttered, struggling to keep her composure. The director leaned in close, his breath hot against her ear.

"Confess," he whispered menacingly. "Tell the world what you've done."

"Done? I haven't done anything!" she insisted, her voice cracking under the strain of her fear.

"Wrong answer," he growled, pulling out a knife from his jacket and brandishing it with a twisted grin. Her eyes widened at the sight of the cold, gleaming steel, her mind racing as she tried to come up with a way to save herself from this nightmare.

"Please," she whispered, her voice trembling with desperation. "I swear I don't know what you're talking about. You've got the wrong person."

"Wrong person?" The director scoffed, circling around her like a vulture closing in on its prey. "No, no, I'm quite certain. See," he paused, tapping the knife against his lips, "It really isn't your fault. I understand that. I'm not an unreasonable man. I'm aware, very much aware, that you've found yourself in an impossible position." He let out a theatrical sigh. "You see, I wouldn't normally ask for a confession, but... as it is, tastes change. The audience demands something new. It's all quite dreary. So.... See this?" he asked, twirling the blade between his fingers with unsettling ease. "This is your ticket to redemption—your chance to cleanse your soul before you leave this world. So confess, dear. You'll never have another chance."

"I... confess what?"

"Anything!" he snapped. "Everything. What is your darkest desire? What is your most shameful secret? The fans want to know! Say hello!"

He wiggled the camcorder.

"I... I once stole a candy bar from a convenience store," she muttered, her voice low and shaky. The director's expression twisted into one of disgust.

"That's it? That's your big confession?" he sneered, shaking his head. "You're more boring than I thought. I'm afraid that won't do at all."

He stepped closer, the knife glinting in the dim light. He pressed the knife to her throat, his breath hot against her ear.

"Try again, my dear. Or else..."

The threat hung heavily in the air.

"I... I once cheated on a test," she stammered, her voice barely above a whisper. The director's expression softened slightly.

"That's better," he said, nodding approvingly. "But we need something more scandalous, don't we? Something that will shock the viewers and make them tune in next week."

He paused, considering her for a moment before continuing. "I can start. I'll show you how. My darkest secret? Would you like to know?"

He smirked as she gave the faintest shakes of her head, but she was too terrified to be vocal. He enjoyed the terror so much that, for a moment, he simply waited, letting the question dangle, savoring her fear and confusion.

"I'll tell you anyway," he said, his grin widening. "I killed my first wife. No one knows, not even the police. I got away with it."

The words hung in the air like a noose around her neck.

"I have to go to the bathroom," she blurted out suddenly, her mind clearly racing for an excuse to leave the room. The director's eyes narrowed suspiciously.

"Nice try, but you're not going anywhere," he said, moving to stand in front of her. "We have unfinished business here. If you won't confess willingly, then we'll do this the hard way."

As the cold steel pressed against her throat, her eyes filled with tears of terror and desperation. The reality of her impending death loomed, leaving her gasping for breath as she choked out one final plea.

"Please... I swear... I don't know anything..."

Just as the director's grip tightened, a sudden explosion of glass shattered the tense silence. The cellar windows imploded, shards flying through the air like deadly confetti.

"Wha—?" the director growled, his knife momentarily forgotten as he swiveled towards the source of the chaos.

"Get down!" a voice boomed from outside, powerful and commanding. "FBI! FBI!"

A blinding flash filled the room, followed by a deafening bang that left the director's ears ringing. He squeezed his eyes shut, disoriented.

"Hands behind your head!" another voice shouted, accompanied by the sound of heavy boots pounding on the concrete floor.

The director just stood there, frozen in place, blinking but hardly seeing anything except shapes. A grenade. A flashbang grenade.

His mind processed this information slowly, and he found his mouth opening and closing in awe.

What the hell was going on here?

His ears were ringing, and he spotted two large, male figures bursting through the cellar door. Both of them had guns raised.

"Drop the knife!" screamed the smaller, more compact one.

The taller one said, "Sweet camera. Mind if I—?" The lanky agent reached out, plucked the camera from its tripod, then slammed it into the director's stomach. He doubled over in pain, gasping at the ground.

This-this couldn't be happening. It wasn't supposed to be possible. This was a *closed set!*

The director was still disoriented and hadn't realized he'd hit the cold concrete until he tried to move his arm and found it pinned under his own body. He lay there, gasping.

The Prodigy had done this. He felt certain of it.

He wasn't sure how, wasn't sure why, but the Prodigy had caused all of this.

Inwardly, even laying on the ground, his temper raged. He snarled, his hand tight on the knife as his vision was still blurred.

He could hear her sobbing in relief.

He clutched the knife, his muscles tensing.

"Do it, big guy," said a drawling voice. "Go for it. Try and stab her. Here, let me help—she's right behind ya. Go for it."

There was something in that voice. Something not just goading but deadly.

An implicit threat.

Try and see what happens.

The director still couldn't quite see. He wasn't sure what was going on around him, but one thing was certain.

He didn't want to tempt the owner of that voice.

So he relaxed his grip on the knife, and it clattered loosely onto the floor.

"Alright, Lenny," said the drawl. "Figure it goes without saying, but your ass is under arrest."

CHAPTER 16

Artemis stood by the police vehicle as the two agents shoved Lenny 'The Lemon' Bodkins towards the car.

Other FBI agents were swarming the place. Paramedics were helping a crying woman out of the basement towards a waiting ambulance, speaking to her in gentle tones.

Artemis' heart went out towards the sobbing woman. She frowned as her gaze moved back towards Mr. Bodkins.

She stifled a yawn.

It was late. And her next two tournament games were tomorrow morning.

She shook her head, refocusing. It was strange the things the mind would suggest in order to comfort a soul in troubling situations.

Lenny Bodkins was shaking his head but didn't say a word as he was pushed towards the police car.

"Not much of a Chatty Cathy, are you?" Forester asked.

He shoved Lenny towards the back door. Artemis stepped aside, providing a wide berth.

"Wait!" Lenny said, suddenly. He was staring directly at Artemis, his eyes like saucers.

"No—No waiting, big guy. Get in!"

But Lenny ignored Forester.

There, standing on the brightly illuminated suburban streets, with more and more neighbors craning out their doors or peering through the curtains in his direction, Lenny almost seemed to bask in the attention.

The spotlight.

A small smile played in the corners of his lips.

"You're the Ghost Killer's daughter," he said.

Artemis sighed, brushing a strand of hair out of her eyes. She'd known that her notoriety extended into the seedier parts of the world.

She supposed it made sense that a man from the Seattle suburbs who'd killed women over the last decade was also familiar with another active killer.

"You search yourself online, don't you," she said, inferring much from this comment.

He didn't reply to this.

Cameron had stopped shoving the man into the backseat now, though, he kept a hand on the killer's shoulder. Instead, Cameron just watched, realizing that the suspect was talking now.

Artemis studied Bodkins' face.

He wasn't a handsome man, and his eyes were as bulging as they'd been in his DMV photo. His gaunt, almost skeletal, features looked even more emaciated than they had in his picture.

He walked with a bit of a duck waddle and was clearly bow-legged.

The gangly, awkward man watched her intently.

"Do you think this will be on the news?" he whispered, excitement in his eyes.

"I don't know," Artemis said, thinking quickly. This was one killer. His tag name online was the dirextor. But they wanted the second one as well.

Another man was out there, also active.

And so she said, "If we'd caught the Prodigy, maybe. But you? I doubt it."

He stared at her as if she'd slapped him.

"The Prodigy?" he whispered.

"Mhmm," she said, keeping her tone indifferent to him. She wasn't even looking in his direction now.

The non-verbals were powerful—communicating rejection, disgust, indifference.

She could see him tensing. Forester gave a little warning growl, his fingers digging into the man's shoulder.

But Bodkins exclaimed, "The Prodigy isn't anywhere near as good as me! He's an amateur, a newcomer!"

"I hear he has actual taste," Artemis said. "He knows angles. Lightning. Story. I hear he's better looking than you. Do you agree?"

She looked at him.

"The Prodigy is a nothing! I bet you it's a collective. A group of people. Yes. I bet the murder was staged!" he exclaimed.

"Not like yours," Forester probed.

"No!" he snapped. "I don't have help. I did it myself."

Artemis stared at the man. He was brazenly admitting to his crimes, but she realized it made sense. He wasn't motivated by his own freedom; he wanted fame.

She said, "You've never met the Prodigy?"

Could they really be completely out of contact with each other? Despite their competition online, despite the similarities in their crimes...

He hesitated, eyes narrowing. For a moment, it seemed as if a flash of sanity crossed his expression. The night was still illuminated by strobing lights from the emergency vehicles. The sound of the woman sobbing could still be heard from the direction of the paramedic's ambulance.

At this sound, Lenny glanced over and swallowed as if savoring something.

Forester took the opportunity to step forward and 'accidentally' drive his knee into the man's groin.

"Whoops," Cameron said as Lenny buckled over with a wincing yelp.

When he looked up, he was glaring at them, his eyes reflecting the strobing lights.

"No one knows him!" he snapped. "But they'll know me. Everyone will know my name!"

"I think you're lying," Artemis said. "I think you know the Prodigy.

She was fishing again.

But his reaction sent chills down her spine.

He smirked.

"You don't know either, do you?" His lips peeled back like a lemon's skin to reveal his teeth. "You're scared, aren't you? I inspired him, you know. His first video was a tribute to me!"

He was clutching between his legs where he'd been kneed, but the hunched, protective stance became sinister as his face cracked in a maniacal grin.

Artemis was beginning to believe him.

He didn't know who the other killer was.

He didn't know the identity of his dark web competition. But beyond that, everything in his answers and attitude confirmed their fears. The Prodigy was real. Not simply a different name dirextor used for his new projects.

She shivered at the thought. This meant there was another murderer out there. Someone else who was targeting the innocent.

"You have to know something," she said quietly.

"Oh? Like what?" he snapped.

"This can go easy for you, or difficult," she began.

Forester leaned in menacingly as if Artemis' words were a prearranged cue for him to follow.

The director snorted, head resting against the cold metal of the police car, his body framed in the open door.

"Please," the self-admitted killer replied. "You're not even doing it right. I know how to invoke fear. You're pedestrian. There's nothing you have. Your hands are tied. I am the one who is really unfettered."

"Big word unfettered," Cameron said. "Does that mean handcuffed?"

The man ignored Cameron's jibe, his eyes fixed on Artemis. "I'll tell you what," he said, his voice low and husky. "You don't strike me the same as these lummoxes, are you?"

She just frowned at him.

He nodded, grinning. "I remember. A chess player. Your father must've been a very, very smart man."

"Are you trying to compliment yourself by complimenting another killer?" she said softly.

He didn't seem perturbed by being called out. Instead, he just shrugged with some indifference.

"Why don't we see just how clever you are, hmm? I don't know the Prodigy, but I know someone who does."

"Who?"

"I'll give you a clue. A riddle, if you will. If you solve it, you'll find what you're looking for. And if you don't..." He trailed off, his eyes glinting dangerously. "Well, let's just say I won't be the only one you'll have to worry about."

Artemis felt a shiver run down her spine. She knew that dealing with this man would be dangerous, but she had no other choice.

"Fine," she said, her voice steady. "What's the clue?"

The man smiled, his lips curving into a sinister grin. "The clue is this," he said. "I am always hungry, I must always be fed. The finger I touch will soon turn red. What am—?"

"Fire."

The director glowered at Artemis' interruption, but she only folded her arms and gave a disappointed shake of her head. "I'm sorry, did you want to finish?"

Grinding his teeth, the director took a sharp breath, looking away and muttering something about 'dramatic timing' under his breath.

"So is that the whole clue?" Artemis asked simply. "A fire... what does that mean?"

The director gave a petulant shrug. "You're so clever. *You* figure it out." Without another word, he flung himself into the back-seat of the cop car with the resigned pessimism of a teenager being driven to school.

Forester slammed the door shut, leaving Wade, Artemis, and himself standing out on the sidewalk.

The sirens of the ambulance wailed as the vehicle pulled away, but Artemis only faintly heard it. She was trying to puzzle out what Lemon had meant by his clue, but her mind felt muddled and her thoughts unresponsive.

She was taxed. Physically and mentally. Giving the ambulance a final look, Artemis offered up a small prayer for the woman in the back.

The thought of praying reminded her of Dr. Bryant and the apparent conflict she'd been having with Wade. Had the two of them been dating? The fact that her brain was struggling with idle gossip told her how tired she really was.

Her mind was flitting from thought to thought, and she could barely keep her eyes open.

Forester glanced at her. "Fire?"

"Think he's bullshitting us?" Wade said.

Artemis shook her head, troubled. "No," she whispered, staring through the window at the profile of the serial killer. "His rivalry with the Prodigy is real. It'll bruise his ego if he's caught and his rival isn't. I think he gave us a real clue."

"What type of clue?"

"I don't know," she said softly, yawning.

"Maybe you should get some rest," Forester said. "I can drive you back. Wade, you got the asshole extraordinaire?"

In answer, Wade merely gave an affirmative grunt and made his way to the front of the vehicle.

Forester turned now, glancing at Artemis and hooking his arm through hers. He led her away from the police vehicles toward another car that had been left idling on the side of the road. A drop-off for the agents.

Artemis slipped into the front seat, and Forester went to the wheel.

"Back to your place?" he said.

She glanced at him, nodding vaguely. "What is it you wanted to tell me?" she said, as they began to drive away from the crime scene.

"Nothing."

"You're still not going to say?"

"It's not worth it yet, Art."

She sighed. "I want to know."

He glanced at her, and for a moment, he almost looked nervous.

"What?"

He rubbed his chin. "You might not like it."

"Like what?"

Finally, he turned to look at her, still driving, but with his eyes on her face. It made her uncomfortable whenever he did this, but she was too curious to force him to focus.

He said, "I think we should bail."

"What?"

"On this place. Seattle. The US. I think we should move."

"Like... move move?"

"Yeah."

She stared at him.

"What?"

"That's not what I was expecting."

He shrugged. "I've been thinking about it. We all have baggage. Hell, serial killers recognize you, Art."

"What about Helen? My father?" she said in the ghost of a whisper.

"Exactly! Them too. They need a fresh start. There are some nice countries with some really nice extradition laws."

She stared at him. "Aren't you supposed to be an FBI agent?"

"Yeah, but I do that mostly to help my aunt." He shrugged. "Besides, I've been thinking I need a change of scenery anyway."

Artemis sat there, frowning. "Where are you thinking?"

"I hear Turkey is nice this time of year," he said. "Istanbul or Ankara."

"Wow. You know your stuff."

"Did you know there's a town in Turkey called Batman? No shit."

"No, I didn't."

Forester's fingers flexed on the steering wheel, and he leaned back. "So?" he said nervously. "We could all get a fresh start. You got a ton of cash now. It'd be the perfect time to bail. Besides... Harmony Schmidt is still looking into you."

"Who?"

"The agent assigned to tail you. I've been doing some digging. She's got a hell of a lot of eyeballs on you, Art. Had your phone tapped."

Artemis froze.

"Don't worry, I turned it off."

She relaxed briefly. "But... this woman... she's still coming after me?"

Forester nodded once. "Like I'm saying... we can bail. So?" He looked at her, an eager light in his eyes. "What about it? Turkish beaches and sunlight? We can eat kebab seaside."

Artemis sat in silence for a moment, considering Forester's proposal. Turkey did sound appealing, especially given the current state of her life. She was tired of constantly looking over her shoulder, always in fear that someone was following her. A fresh start could be just what she needed.

"I don't know," she said finally. "It's a big decision."

"I know," Forester said. "But think about it. We could have a new life, a new identity. We could start over."

Artemis nodded slowly, still lost in thought. She had never been one to shy away from taking risks, but this felt different. It felt like a major life decision, one that could either turn out to be the best thing that ever happened to her or a complete disaster.

"I'll think about it," she said finally. "But I need some time to consider. And I'll have to talk to Helen."

"Sure," Forester said with a smile. "Take all the time you need."

Artemis smiled back at him, feeling grateful for his support.

As they drove down the quieting streets of Seattle, Artemis couldn't help but feel a sense of unease.

It was late. Very late, but murderers had an odd habit of operating in the dark.

The director, dirextor, was in custody.

But the Prodigy was still out there.

And of the two, the second one seemed the more dangerous.

She shivered now, rubbing her hands against her arms. She leaned over, pressing her fingers against Forester's forearm as if simply looking for something tangible to touch.

The warmth of his skin gave her a brief sense of ease.

But all the while, she couldn't shake the images of the murder of Jessica Parker.

The woman had been terrified.

Suddenly, Forester's phone began to ring.

He frowned, and Artemis glanced over sharply.

"Yeah?" he said.

She waited, and as she watched, a peculiar change occurred in Forester's features.

The blood seemed to leave his face. "You're sure? When? Yeah... she's with me. I'll tell her. Yeah—I'll tell her. No, don't be an ass."

He hung up.

"Who was that?" she said instinctively.

"My aunt."

"What does Agent Grant want?" Artemis asked softly, a cold dread slowly coiling in her chest.

"We think... the Prodigy may have taken another. He's live streaming it right now on the same website."

Artemis stared. "...really?" She began reaching for her phone, but Forester's hand shot out, catching her wrist.

"You don't want to see that."

"What.... why?"

"Trust me, Art."

"What's going on?"

Something in his tone had shifted. There was something there that made her stomach turn.

Forester loosed a soft sigh, and then he murmured, "It's Jamie Kramer, Artemis. The killer has Jamie Kramer."

CHAPTER 17

Confusion swirled through his mind like an unwelcome fog, and for a few disorienting moments, Jamie Kramer had no idea where he was or why he felt such fear clawing at the edges of his consciousness.

As the haze of sleep slowly dissipated, he became aware of the raw ache in his wrists, and when he tried to move his hands, he found that they were tied tightly together behind his back. Panic bubbled up inside him, and his breathing grew rapid and shallow, each breath feeling like a desperate gasp for air.

He wriggled his fingers, trying to loosen the bindings, but the pain only intensified as the rough rope dug deeper into his tender flesh. He bit back a cry of agony, realizing that struggling would only cause further damage to his already bruised and battered hands.

As he strained against the ropes, Jamie's eyes adjusted to the faint glow of light reflecting off the swirling blue patterns about twenty feet below him. He became aware of his surroundings—the heavy scent of chlorine filled his nostrils as if trying to leave no doubt that he was near an indoor pool. The moist air clung to his skin, making the rope feel even more abrasive than before. He could hear the distant and eerie hum of the water filtration system, punctuated by the occasional dripping sound echoing throughout the room.

He shifted some more and the floor wobbled.

It was then he realized where he was.

Tied to a pole at the top of a diving board.

The diving board jutted out, over the water.

He shivered, feeling a prickle of anxiety mingling with vertigo as his whole body abruptly locked. Every small movement felt larger now, as if a wrong breath would send him plummeting, still bound, into the water below.

"Hello?" Jamie called out, hoping against hope that someone might be nearby—a janitor, a late-night swimmer, anyone who could help. But there was no response, just the haunting silence that seemed to amplify his own ragged breaths.

As the ominous silence stretched on, Jamie's thoughts tumbled back to the night. His memory came back in pieces, like a broken kaleidoscope reassembling shard by shard. He could almost hear the shattering of glass as the intruder burst into his home, the sharp tang of adrenaline flooding his senses. In that moment, everything had become a blur of motion and instinct—furniture overturned, the desperate scramble for a weapon, anything to fend off the shadowy figure.

Amidst the chaos, one thought surged above all others: Sophie. His younger sister lived under his roof now. They'd been orphaned the previous year under tragic circumstances, and he'd attempted to carve out a new life for the both of them.

Now, though, terror filled him, nipping at his mind.

Someone had attacked him. Someone had knocked him unconscious.

Where the hell was Sophie?

Just as Jamie felt a new wave of fear, a booming voice shattered the silence. The distorted sound reverberated through the air, echoing off the tiled walls of the indoor pool.

"Ah, you're awake," the voice taunted over a megaphone. "I was starting to get bored waiting for you."

Jamie's heart skipped a beat, fear seizing his chest. He squinted into the dimly lit room, searching for the source of the voice but finding nothing but shadows.

"Who are you?" he demanded, his own words sounding feeble in comparison. "What do you want?"

"Confess," the voice replied, cold and unyielding. "Confess your sins, and maybe—just maybe—I'll let you live."

"Confess? I don't know what you're talking about!" Jamie cried out, panic-stricken. His mind raced, trying to make sense of the situation. What could he possibly confess to that might save him?

"Please," he begged, desperation creeping into his voice. "I don't know what you want from me. Just let me go, please."

"Such a pity," the voice said mockingly. "I had hoped you'd be smarter than this. But no matter. You can't keep your secrets forever."

Jamie's thoughts whirled chaotically, grasping at anything that might help him understand what was happening. He knew he had to stay strong, not just for himself, but for Artemis too. She would never give up, he reminded himself, so neither could he.

"Look," Jamie said, forcing the tremor from his voice. "I don't know who you are or what you think I've done, but you've got the wrong person. I haven't done anything worth confessing, I swear!"

The voice remained silent for a moment, as though contemplating Jamie's words. The oppressive atmosphere grew heavier, pressing down on Jamie like a crushing weight.

"Time is running out," the voice finally warned. "Choose wisely or suffer the consequences."

Jamie's mind raced, his fear and confusion threatening to overwhelm him. He knew he had to find a way to turn the situation around, but how? As the seconds ticked by, Jamie sank further into despair, fearing that his fate was already sealed.

"Please," he whispered one last time, his plea hanging in the air like a frail thread of hope. "Please let me go."

Before Jamie could respond, a red dot, a laser sight, appeared on his chest. His breathing hitched as he stared at the unwavering dot, its crimson glow offering a chilling contrast against the pale skin of his exposed torso. It was then that he realized what the voice intended—they were threatening to shoot him, and with every passing second, the threat loomed ever closer.

"Last chance, Jamie," the voice said, its menace palpable even through the distortion of the megaphone. "Confess or say goodbye."

"Please," he choked out, the word barely audible as his thoughts raced. He couldn't think, couldn't breathe—all that existed was the laser sight and the cold, malevolent voice behind it. Sophie's face swam before his eyes, a reminder of what was at stake.

"Please," he whispered again, desperation lacing his voice as he fought to find the strength to hold onto hope. "Don't do this."

The red laser sight remained fixed on his chest, a burning reminder of the danger he faced.

"Tick-tock, Jamie," the voice taunted over the megaphone, its source still hidden from view. "Time's running out."

"Look, I don't know what you want me to say!" Jamie yelled, frustration gnawing at him. "I can't confess to something I don't understand! Please, just tell me what you want!"

"Ah, poor, confused Jamie," the voice mocked. "Tell me about Artemis Blythe."

Jamie froze.

"A-Artemis? What about her?"

"Tell me about the Ghost Killer!"

Jamie went stiff as a board, his mouth open.

"Confess!" the voice echoed.

Jamie knew Artemis' family secret. It was the reason they'd broken up. He hadn't betrayed her confidence, but he simply couldn't trust her judgement. Artemis' sister, Helen, was deranged. She'd been a menace, and as much as Artemis believed her sister could be cured, Jamie didn't share the same sentiment.

Now, though, he realized the voice coming through on the megaphone was taunting him.

It wanted this from him.

The truth about the Blythe sisters.

"I... I don't know what you're talking about!" he yelled. He couldn't betray Artemis. Not even now. But again, an image of his sister, Sophie, flashed through his mind. Where was she? Was she safe?

"I said confess!" the voice howled, angry now. "You're testing my patience, Jamie."

Jamie's mind raced, his fear and confusion threatening to overwhelm him. He knew he had to find a way to turn the situation around but how? He couldn't let Sophie down. He couldn't let Artemis down. He had to think of something, and fast.

The laser sight continued to hover on his chest, a constant reminder of the danger he was in. He could feel sweat beading on his forehead, his heart pounding in his chest. He had to find a way out of this.

"Please," he said, his voice shaking. "I don't know what you want from me. I swear I haven't done anything wrong."

The voice on the megaphone remained silent for a moment, as though weighing Jamie's words. Jamie held his breath, waiting for the voice to speak again. He could feel his heart racing, his mind whirling.

"You're playing ignorant. Choose. Or die."

The red light on his chest was no longer wavering. It had gone still.

A second later, Jamie realized it wasn't the light that had stilled but his lungs. He'd forgotten to take another breath.

He couldn't tell... He couldn't betray Artemis.

He realized there was no way out. He was still disoriented, still panicked, but he cared too much about Artemis to give in.

So what choice did he have?

With a heavy heart, Jamie closed his eyes and inhaled deeply, feeling the damp air fill his lungs. He had made his decision, and there was no turning back now. His heart pounded against his ribs like a wild animal trapped in a cage, but he refused to let fear rule him any longer.

"Fine," he whispered, his voice barely audible over the echoing sound of water lapping at the pool's edge. "Do what you have to do."

"Bravery doesn't suit you, Jamie," the voice sneered, its distorted tone reverberating around the empty room.

The red laser sight remained fixed on his chest, and he braced himself for the gunshot that would end it all. He imagined Artemis' determined eyes—one blue like moonlit frost, the other hazel gold—glistening with unshed tears as she learned of his fate. He hoped she would understand why he'd chosen to protect her.

Seconds stretched into an eternity, yet the gunshot never came. Instead, the laser light blinked out, leaving him in near-total darkness once more.

The oppressive darkness of the indoor pool room seemed to close in on Jamie, making it difficult to breathe. The damp air carried the pungent scent of chlorine and echoed with faint dripping sounds. He could feel the coarse rope binding his wrists, chafing against his skin as he shifted in his seat.

"Please," Jamie whispered into the void, his voice cracking with desperation. "Just let me go."

He strained to hear any sign of the megaphone man's presence, but there was only silence. The unsettling quiet filled him with dread, and he realized that the killer might be watching him from the shadows, observing his every move.

"Let's talk about this," he tried again, attempting to keep his fear in check. "Maybe we can come to some sort of agreement."

But the voice was gone.

The megaphone had gone silent.

What did it mean?

Surely the psycho hadn't given up...

There was something equally ominous in the silence. His thoughts moved to Sophie once more.

And then to Artemis.

This was all because of her, wasn't it?

He'd known Artemis' life was a troubled one, but his own father had been tainted by the Ghost Killer. Or at least, who he'd thought was the Ghost Killer. His mother was dead because of it.

Artemis and Jamie had broken up because of it.

And now, Sophie was in danger...

He was about to die.

He scowled, realizing his mind was trying to play tricks. Trying to build a case against Artemis, to justify betraying her.

But he refused to give in.

He scowled deeply, snarling to himself, and continued to work at the ropes binding him to the pole.

But he didn't have to understand or justify anything. The only thing he had left to do was escape.

CHAPTER 18

If such a thing were possible, the buzz at the precinct had only intensified, but Artemis walked like a zombie, moving slowly at Forester's side, her mind like molasses. She felt as if she were sleeping.

Her gaze was glued to the phone in Forester's hand. He was close against her as if providing support or perhaps fearful her legs might buckle, and he'd have to catch her.

Artemis' heart raced as she stared at the video feed, her breath hitching in her throat. Her mismatched eyes were wide with panic, locked onto the image of Jamie tied to the diving board pole at the pool.

"Jamie," she whispered, her voice barely audible above the cacophony of the room.

The precinct was alive with activity, a frenzied chaos that left no corner untouched. Officers sprinted back and forth, barking orders and updating each other on new developments. Multiple televisions projected the live video, casting an eerie glow over the space, amplifying the urgency pulsating through the air. The actual killer had managed to make this personal, and Artemis couldn't shake the feeling that she was the intended target.

The godfather's son was still in custody. So half the noise and chaos was due to this.

But the development with the live-streamed video was the secondary impetus.

Everything was in an uproar.

Artemis tried to focus on Forester's words as he spoke to them, but the images of Jamie bound and helpless refused to leave her mind. She couldn't help but feel responsible, the weight of guilt settling heavily on her shoulders.

"Look for any clues in the video feed," Forester suggested. "Anything that might give us an idea of where they are."

"Right," Artemis nodded, swallowing hard as she forced herself to concentrate on the task at hand. With her photographic memory, she could recall every detail of the footage with striking clarity. As she mentally scanned the scene, the sounds of the precinct faded into the background, replaced by the pounding of her own heartbeat.

Artemis' chest tightened, breaths coming in shallow gasps as the video feed continued to play. Her vision blurred, the panicked voices of the precinct merging into a cacophony of confusion and fear. The knot in her stomach twisted tighter, guilt gnawing at her insides.

"Artemis," Forester said, his voice cutting through the noise. He placed a hand on her shoulder, grounding her for a moment. "Breathe with me, okay? In and out."

She tried to focus on the sound of his voice, but her thoughts raced, each one more terrifying than the last. Jamie's life was in danger, the clock ticking down on their chances of saving him.

"Artemis, stay with me. You can do this," Forester urged, his tone firm yet supportive. "I need you to find something, anything, that could help us locate Jamie."

"Okay," she choked out, forcing herself to take a deep breath. With trembling hands, she wiped away the tears from her cheeks and turned her attention back to the video feed.

"Good. That's it," Forester encouraged, his hand remaining a comforting presence on her shoulder.

As Artemis scanned the footage, her heart pounded in her ears, drowning out the chaos around her. She felt a sudden surge of determination, fueled by the desire to protect Jamie and put an end to the terror they were both facing.

But even as her resolve rose, there was a barking order issued by a sergeant near them. A cop knocked over a pile of papers. Someone was shouting in a distant interrogation room.

The chaos was too much. Artemis' stomach was tight, and a panic attack was threatening to rise within her again.

"Forester, I need a moment," Artemis muttered, her voice barely audible amidst the frenzy of the precinct. Her panic attack had subsided to manageable levels, but she still felt the residual effects of anxiety coursing through her veins.

"Of course."

"Thank you," she said, grateful for his unwavering support. With a shaky exhale, she stumbled towards the nearest bathroom.

As she closed the door behind her, Artemis relished the sudden quiet that enveloped her, the chaos of the precinct muffled by the barrier between them. The dim lighting provided a stark contrast to the harsh fluorescents outside, offering a small reprieve for her frazzled nerves.

"Get it together, Artemis," she whispered to herself, her voice echoing slightly in the empty room. "You can't help Jamie if you're falling apart."

Her heart continued to race as she fumbled for the light switch, plunging the room into complete darkness. She leaned against the cold tiles of the wall, feeling a strange comfort in the void. It was there, in the darkness, where she could shut out the world and find solace, even if just for a moment.

"Focus on your breath," she instructed herself, trying to follow the same techniques she used to quell her anxiety. Inhaling deeply, she allowed the darkness to envelop her, to embrace her like a protective cocoon.

"Exhale," she whispered, slowly releasing the breath she had been holding. As the air left her lungs, so too did some of the tension that had coiled tightly within her muscles.

With her back pressed against the cold tiles, Artemis' mind raced uncontrollably. She couldn't help but imagine the worst possible outcomes for Jamie. Her chest tightened as a vivid image of him struggling, bound to the diving board pole, surfaced in her thoughts. The guilt that gnawed at her intensified with each horrifying scenario.

"God, what if he's hurt... or worse?" she muttered under her breath, clenching her fists tightly. "All because someone wants to get to me?" She knew that panicking wouldn't save Jamie; she needed a clear mind to figure out how to help him.

She closed her eyes and focused on her breathing, inhaling deeply through her nose. She imagined the air filling her lungs like a balloon expanding within her chest. Then she exhaled slowly, feeling the warmth of her breath against her lips.

"Okay, think," she whispered.

As she continued to practice the breathing technique, Artemis gradually felt a semblance of control returning.

As the darkness of the bathroom enveloped her, Artemis leaned against the cold tiled wall, allowing herself a moment to gather her thoughts.

"Focus," she muttered under her breath, her voice echoing faintly in the small room. "Remember the video."

Artemis closed her eyes, concentrating on the live feed she had seen just minutes ago. The image came into focus with striking clarity: Jamie's terrified expression, the frayed ropes binding him to the diving board pole, the menacing shadows that surrounded him.

"Details," she whispered. "I need details."

She mentally zoomed in on the environment surrounding her ex. The pool's shimmering surface came into view, followed by the cracked vinyl beneath Jamie's feet. A faint smell of chlorine filled her nostrils as she imagined herself standing there, searching for clues to his location.

"Artemis?" Forester's concerned voice called through the door, making her jump. "Are you alright in there?"

"Y-yeah," she stammered, not wanting to reveal the extent of her panic. "I'll be out in a minute."

Concentrate, Artemis thought to herself, focusing once more on the mental image. As she scanned the area, something caught her eye; a barely visible object lurking in the background.

"Wait... what is that?" Her mind raced as she tried to make out the obscured detail. She honed in on it, the mental image growing sharper and clearer.

"Is that... a scoreboard?" Artemis' heart leaped with hope. It was a small detail, but it could be significant. A clue that might lead them straight to Jamie.

"Forester!" she cried, her voice filled with newfound determination. "I think I found something. I'm coming out."

With one last steadying breath, Artemis flipped the light switch, leaving the darkness behind as she stepped out of the bathroom.

She burst through the bathroom door, her eyes wide with a mix of fear and hope. The sudden brightness of the precinct stung her still-adjusting eyes as she rushed to Forester's side.

"What's up, Checkers?" Forester asked, his expression a mix of concern and curiosity.

"Look," she breathed, pointing at the paused video feed on the screen. Her fingers trembled slightly as she traced the outline of the barely visible object in the background. "The scoreboard. It's the same design as the one at the pool where Jamie and I used to go when we were in school."

"Are you sure?" he questioned, squinting at the blurry image.

"Positive," she replied, her dual-colored eyes filled with certainty. "I know that crack, there. It's shaped like an L."

Forester let out a long whistle, tilting his head appreciatively as he leaned in to whisper, "Y'know, you don't have to lie to me anymore. You can just say that you're psychic."

"Let's go," Artemis urged, unable to appreciate the joke with her heart pounding wildly in her chest. She couldn't shake the feeling that time was running out for Jamie.

As they rushed towards the exit, Artemis' mind churned with memories of the pool, the way the chlorine stung her eyes, the echo of laughter bouncing off the tiled walls. She tried to focus on these happier times, but her thoughts were consumed by the darkened room in which Jamie now lay captive.

"Wait." Forester held her back for a moment, near the door. "We need backup. We can't just rush in there."

"Fine," Artemis gritted her teeth, knowing he was right but hating the delay all the same. "But make it quick. Every second counts."

She leaned against the wall, clenching her fists, her body trembling with fear and adrenaline. In her mind, she saw Jamie's anguished face, and she whispered to herself, "You can't die. Don't you dare die!"

Chapter 19

Artemis and Forester sped through the night, following behind the three police cars ahead of them. Sirens blared, lights flashed, and the few trailing vehicles on midnight highways were swept aside.

But something was nagging at Artemis.

Forester glanced at her in the rearview mirror. "What's wrong?" he said.

"Just..." she frowned. "Why would he make it so obvious?"

"Who?"

"The killer. Why would he lure us to such an obvious location? He didn't try to hide it. And if he went after Jamie, it means he knows about me."

"And your father, most likely. My guess is the Ghost Killer attracted the Prodigy to Jamie."

"Yeah..." Artemis swallowed, leaning back in the seat, her body like a coiled spring, adrenaline buzzing through her veins. "Just ... he's smart. He'd know I'd have perfect recall. If he knew about Jamie, he knows about my memory. And he's smarter than the other one."

"What are you suggesting?"

"I think we're going into a trap," she said, looking at Cameron.

Forester frowned, his muscles tensed, his jaw jutting.

"Yeah... can't rule it out," he muttered.

Artemis felt a faint shiver move down her spine as the leading police vehicle veered off onto a familiar exit. She could see the outline of the red brick school ahead. She remembered staying with the Kramer's; remembered that Mrs. Kramer had been the only mother figure she'd ever really had.

But she was dead too, now.

So much death.

Artemis sometimes wanted to escape it all. She thought of Forester's offer.

Briefly, as they sped towards the large, red-brick school building, she thought of leaving it all. Moving to Turkey or South Africa... Turkey's beaches sounded nice; the extradition hostilities were an added bonus.

But...

Would Helen want to? Her father? What about Tommy?

She shivered.

A fresh start for all of them?

Or was she just deluding herself?

The screech of rubber against the road jarred her to the present as the cars ahead of her left streaks of black against the asphalt.

Police officers jumped out of the vehicles in front of the looming, red brick school.

The school looked more like an old manor house than a place overrun with children five days a week. It had a large courtyard with a fountain in the center. The dimly lit windows gave off an eerie vibe as if the building itself was alive and watching them.

"Stay close," Forester warned her, his hand resting on his gun. "We don't know what kind of situation we're walking into."

Artemis nodded, her heart pounding in her chest as they followed the police officers towards the entrance.

"Remember. It could be a trap," she whispered to Forester. "Tell them to be careful."

Forester nodded and took a couple jogging steps forward to address the officer leading the charge.

Artemis' skin prickled as she and Forester followed the police officers deeper into the gothic-style, red-brick school. Each hurried footstep echoed, amplifying the sense of urgency and tension that filled the dimly lit halls. The officers' flashlights cut through the darkness, casting eerie shadows on the walls.

The six police officers, led by the man in body armor with a pencil-thin mustache, moved with a weaponlike precision, as if every motion was calculated.

Artemis couldn't help but feel a strange familiarity as they navigated the labyrinthine corridors. The school's architecture stirred memories of her childhood—the tall arched windows, the ornate ironwork that adorned the staircases, and the way the shadows seemed to crawl along the walls like tendrils reaching out for her, intent on pulling her once more into the past.

As they continued, Artemis noticed how the school had aged since her time there. The once vibrant red bricks were now stained with age and neglect. The floorboards creaked beneath their feet as if protesting the intrusion.

"Listen up, team," said one of the officers, bringing everyone to a halt. "We're approaching the gym up ahead. Eyes out for anything amiss."

Artemis couldn't shake the feeling that something was amiss. The way was clear, doors were open, inviting them in like they were expected.

"Stay close, Artemis," Forester murmured, his voice steady despite the tension that hung heavy in the air.

With every step closer to the gym, the eerie atmosphere of the school seemed to tighten its grip on her.

Now, she spotted the old trophy case. At the end of the hall, two wide double doors were sealed.

The word Gymnasium was painted above the frame.

Just as they passed the trophy case, a shrill ringtone pierced the air. The man in charge, his face pale and beads of sweat forming on his brow, fumbled with his phone before answering.

Artemis stared. A few of the other cops hesitated, frowning at their leader.

Was he taking a phone call in the middle of the damn raid?

Come to think of it...

Artemis frowned. Why had he left his ringtone on, to begin with?

Forester tensed at her side too as the two of them stared at the man in the lead, both of their faces etched with quizzical expressions.

"Hello?" he stammered, his voice shaking with visible anxiety. His eyes flickered nervously around the hallway as if searching for an unseen threat.

Artemis watched him closely, her unease growing by the second. She'd seen people react like this before—cornered, desperate, afraid. And it never ended well.

"Forester," she whispered, tugging gently at his sleeve to get his attention. "Something's not right."

The man in charge looked pale. He was breathing heavily. "I understand," he said into the phone's receiver. "Yes... yes, I know."

The man in charge ended his call abruptly, his hand visibly trembling as he gripped the phone tightly. He looked up at the group, his eyes darting between them as though assessing their reactions.

"Everything okay?" one officer asked hesitantly, his weapon still at the ready.

"Fine," the man in charge said, his voice cracking slightly. "Just a small issue I need to handle later. Let's move."

The officer's nervousness was palpable, emanating off him like a suffocating fog.

"Bullshit," Cameron said sharply, halting the group's progress toward the gym.

The man in charge hesitated, his jaw clenching as he shot a glare back to Forester. "What was that?"

"Bull sh-it," Forester repeated, over-articulating the word as he did. "What was that? What are we walking into?"

The mustached leader's eyes narrowed, glancing between Forester and the remaining cops as he seemed to weigh his options. A bead of sweat trickled down his temple, betraying his anxiety.

"Fine," the man relented, swallowing hard. "It was an emergency line... from my wife."

"Your wife?" Cameron repeated, his voice steady despite the suspicion creeping into his eyes. "What did she want?"

"It's... it's a family emergency," he managed to say, his voice wavering slightly.

The other cops surrounding him were eyeing him with uncertainty.

Another man inched forward, whispering something to the first.

But the one in charge just shook his head.

"Jameson, take Reeves and Austin and cover the parking lot."

Forester frowned. "You sure that's a good idea?"

"Can't give the bastard an escape route," replied the officer in charge. He pushed his chest out, his eyes flashing, his lip trembling.

The man in question, Jameson, hesitated. "You sure, sir?"

"Are you questioning a damn order!" snapped the officer.

Artemis watched as Jameson's face fell, the color draining from his cheeks. He shook his head and nodded, a defeated expression etched on his face.

The group split, with Jameson leading Reeves and Austin in the direction of the vehicles. This only left three police behind, joining Artemis and Forester as they moved towards the gymnasium.

The leading officer pushed a hand against the sealed door and shook his head. Almost as if relieved. "Locked!" he said.

The man turned back around to find the others all still watching him.

"Well?" Forester said, irritation creeping into his voice. "Are you going to kick it in or should I?"

The cop bit his lip, hesitant. "I..." he trailed off, one hand lingering near his phone while the other wiped the sweat on his forehead trickling down.

"Just get out of the way," Cameron moving to step around the commander.

The officer braced himself, stepping between the Cameron and the door. "No," he said hurriedly. "It's locked, so it's secure. Let's circle around the building and make sure there's nobody else here." He stiffly gestured back the way they'd come, like a kindergarten play approximation of a soldier. "We don't want to be too hasty."

Artemis stepped forward, her gaze narrowing. "You're stalling," she accused. "What aren't you telling us?" Her thoughts moved to Jamie, and her voice was tinged with desperation.

The officer's face turned a deep shade of red, his eyes shifting away from them. He opened his mouth to speak, only to be cut off by Artemis once more.

"Who really called you?" she asked. But the words were hollow. She already knew.

A trap.

The man's face paled. He tensed and in that same moment, he pulled his weapon, fast, and aimed it directly at Artemis' head.

"I'm sorry—but he has my wife."

Artemis went still. The other officers' expressions shifted from confusion to alarm. Forester stepped forward, his hands raised in a gesture of peace.

"Calm down," he said, his voice low and steady. "We don't want anyone to get hurt."

The officer's eyes darted back and forth, flickering with fear and desperation. "I don't have a choice," he said, his voice shaking. "He's got my wife. He's holding her hostage."

Artemis felt a surge of sympathy for the man, but it was quickly overtaken by a sense of urgency. She needed to act fast, before things spiraled out of control.

"Who has your wife?" she asked, her voice sharp. Of course, she knew who. They all did. "Where is she?"

The officer hesitated, his grip on the gun tightening. She could see the fear in his eyes, the desperation. She knew what it was like to feel trapped, to have someone you loved in danger.

She took a hesitant step towards him, fingers outstretched. "Put the gun down," she said softly.

"Sorry," he whispered a final time. And then he squeezed the trigger.

CHAPTER 20

Artemis had been expecting the gunshot.

She'd seen it in his posture, in the desperation in the officer's eyes.

Whatever he'd heard on that phone call had convinced him there was no going back. It didn't matter that he was surrounded by colleagues. It didn't matter that he was facing an FBI agent and CI.

All that mattered was whatever he'd heard on that phone call.

And so as he'd tensed, and as his finger had pulled the trigger, Artemis lunged in. She'd seen Forester do it so many times before, it was like following a blueprint in her mind's eye.

She wasn't sure what possessed her. What had come over her?

But she knew Jamie Kramer was on the other side of those locked doors, in the hands of a sadist.

She flung a hand out as she watched him tense. The faint motion to the side disturbed his aim, if only briefly.

The brief distraction bought her precious time. As he diverted his gun ever so slightly to track the movement of her hand, Artemis came in close.

Her own hand slammed into his wrist.

He let out a shout of pain as her shoulder connected with his sternum.

The man hit the ground with a painful thump! The breath whooshing from his lungs.

The two other police who'd remained behind and witnessed the whole thing, hurried forward, handcuffs at the ready.

Artemis didn't even look as they cuffed their boss, dragging him to his feet. Instead, she turned toward the door, approaching it cautiously. As she appraised the lock, she vaguely heard Forester ordering the other two officers outside.

"We have it in here. Get him secured and figure out where his wife is ASAP. If she's really been taken we need someone on that immediately."

As the footsteps retreated behind them, Forester appeared at Artemis' side, his gun drawn.

"Just you and me, Checkers. Ready?"

Artemis nodded. She tried the handle, ignoring the sound of whimpering and pleading from the former commander disappearing behind her.

The man was clearly desperate to keep his wife safe...

But there was only one person who could stop all of this.

And he was on the other side of this door...

Or was he?

She hesitated, frowning, her hand touching the cool metal of the handle.

What if the Prodigy wasn't even here?

What if he'd lured all of them for some *other* twisted purpose?

She tugged at the door.

Locked.

She cursed under her breath. She'd half-hoped the commander had been lying about that too.

"Step back," Forester commanded.

She did, and Forester's gun snapped up. Two shots and the lock shattered.

Artemis reached out, pushing at the door.

It opened slowly, but Forester held out a hand. And she stopped.

"Check for wires," he said, "Before you push it fully."

She nodded.

Forester was leaning forward, his eye scanning the crack above the door.

After a few moments, he stepped back, lowering his gun.

"All clear," he said, giving her a nod.

Artemis exhaled shakily, nodded once to summon her own resolve, and then pushed the door open, stepping inside.

The scent of chlorine hit her in an instant, wafting over her, and Artemis' eyes scanned the room beyond. The swimming pool glowed blue, lights under the surface illuminating the water. Her eyes snapped to the diving board. She paused, staring at the space above the white, wooden board.

But there was no sign of Jamie or the killer.

Forester stepped up beside her, his gun still drawn as he surveyed the area. His gaze swept over the empty pool, and then up towards the balcony above. He motioned for Artemis to stay put as he crept forward, checking for any signs that someone may have been here recently.

"Looks empty," Forester said quietly as he moved cautiously along the side of the pool.

Artemis and Forester stood at the edge of the old school gym. She tugged on her simple ponytail, scanning the room for any signs of the killer.

The sound of police radios crackled in the distance, but it was clear that their backup was still engaged with the arrest outside the doors, leaving Artemis and Forester to navigate the treacherous waters of this investigation alone. Before either of them could take another step, the lights suddenly went out, plunging the gym into darkness so thick it felt like a physical presence.

"Shit!" Forester cursed, fumbling for a flashlight. The sounds of the police seemed to vanish, swallowed by the oppressive blackness that surrounded them.

In the suffocating darkness, Artemis mentally retraced their steps through the gym, trying to remember the layout of the space. The killer could be anywhere, watching them from the shadows, waiting for the perfect moment to strike.

"Artemis," Forester whispered, his voice an anchor in the dark void surrounding them. "Do you hear that?"

"Wait..." Artemis strained her ears, suddenly aware of a faint noise. Fear sent shivers down her spine but her determination burned even brighter. She couldn't let her fear hold her back. Jamie's life was at stake. "I think I hear something."

"Where?" Forester's voice was tense, laden with unease.

"Over there, by the pool." Artemis took a tentative step forward, her senses heightened in the darkness. Her heart pounded in her chest as she tried to focus on the sound, unsure of what it could mean.

"Stay close," Forester cautioned, his hand finding hers in the blackness. Their fingers intertwined, providing some small measure of comfort amidst the unknown.

The splashing sound grew louder as they approached the edge of the pool, and Artemis caught a brief flicker of light reflecting off the water. It was then that she realized... something was in the pool. Moving slowly, almost... twitching?

"Forester," she gasped, her grip tightening around his hand. "There's someone in the pool!"

"Are you sure? It's so dark..."

"Yes, I'm sure! We need to help them!" Panic and adrenaline fueled her movements as Artemis stepped closer to the edge of the pool, her eyes desperately trying to scan the rippling water, trying to make out any sign of the person in distress as the flashlight cast about erratically.

Artemis squinted, her heart pounding in her chest. She tried to make out the struggling figure in the water as Forester circled the pool, his light periodically flitting away as he scanned the area around them.

There. The flickering of the blue light cast eerie shadows across the surface, but it was enough for her to see a flash of familiar features.

"Jamie," she breathed, her voice barely audible as the horror of recognition washed over her. He was bound and gagged, helplessly trying to keep his head above water. A surge of anger mixed with fear coursed through her veins, and yet there was no sign of the mastermind behind this twisted scene.

Suddenly the flashlight twisted away, plunging the entire room into darkness.

"Forester, I need the light. It's Jamie!" she shouted, turning to look for her partner, but he was nowhere to be found. The darkness seemed to swallow him whole, leaving her feeling stranded and alone. "Forester!" she called again, more urgently this time, but only silence answered her.

And now she knew it was a trap.

It had all been staged.

'Staged,' a distant part of Artemis' mind noted the ironically appropriate word. Quite literally a performance.

For a moment, Artemis considered running around the pool to where she last saw her partner. But Jamie was drowning, and as much as it hurt, Artemis had to trust Forester was taking care of himself, whatever had happened.

"Artemis... focus," she whispered to herself, forcing her thoughts to shift back to the task at hand—saving Jamie.

She hesitated for a heartbeat, then hurled herself into the pool, the cold water swallowing her whole. She could feel the pressure building in her ears as she sank deeper, the icy water biting at her skin like a thousand needles. Her heart pounded in her chest, echoing her desperation, and her thoughts raced with equal intensity.

Her hands reached out, grasping for any sign of him in the watery dark. Finally, her fingers brushed against the rough texture of rope, telling her that she had found him. Relief washed over her for a moment, but there was no time to celebrate.

As she struggled to untie the knots, the ropes seemed to fight back against her, unwilling to release their captive. Artemis' lungs burned with the need for air, but she couldn't abandon Jamie now. The urgency of the situation fueled her resolve, and she kept at her task, her fingers working frantically.

The knots finally loosened, and Artemis managed to pry the ropes free from his wrists and ankles. His body began to float upwards, and she propelled them both towards the surface, kicking hard and fast.

Finally, they broke the surface, gasping for air. Artemis clung to Jamie, her relief mingling with the lingering fear that still gripped her. Water droplets skimmed her face as she gasped desperately, treading in the cold liquid.

"Jamie, can you hear me?" she asked, her voice shaking. Chlorine stung her nostrils. She held onto Jamie tightly, making sure he was safe, but her mind was racing with thoughts of the killer.

Where was Forester? Why had he disappeared? Was he in danger too?

Artemis scanned the dark gym, trying to see past the shadows that surrounded her.

Her heart pounded in her chest as she led Jamie to the edge of the pool, their movements slowed by the water that resisted them. She kept one arm around him, partially supporting his weight while he coughed and sputtered. The adrenaline coursing through her veins made her hands shake.

"Almost there," she muttered, both to herself and to Jamie. Her relief was palpable, but each passing second felt like a lifetime. Every moment they remained in the water was another chance for something to go horribly wrong.

Reaching the side of the pool, Artemis braced herself against the cold tiles, gritting her teeth.

Jamie was still unresponsive, his head lolled to the side.

She needed to get him out of the pool, but he was heavier than her.

"Forester!" she cried out.

Again, no reply, and now her panic was redirected to this new horror. Where was Cameron?

She was still stuck, treading water.

She grit her teeth, summoning what reserves of endurance remained.

With a sudden burst of energy, Artemis took the edge of the pool with one hand, letting out a cry of exertion as she pulled Jamie's waterlogged shoulder with the other. Inch by agonizing inch, she managed to hoist Jamie out of the pool and onto the hard, unforgiving tiles.

Artemis frantically checked his pulse, her fingers trembling as she pressed them against his neck. A faint throb met her touch, and she breathed a sigh of relief. He was alive, but barely. She couldn't waste any more time here, not with the killer still on the loose.

Artemis pulled Jamie away from the edge of the pool, her arms straining under his weight. She dragged him across the floor, her eyes flicking around the room as she scanned for any sign of Forester. But there was no sign of him in the oppressive dark. The flashlights were nowhere to be seen.

"Forester!" she shouted, her voice echoing in the empty gym. There was no response. She was alone, with a half-drowned Jamie in her arms, and a killer on the loose.

Artemis set Jamie down on the floor, her eyes never leaving his face. He was still unconscious, but his breathing was steady. She needed to get him to a hospital, fast.

Suddenly, something tapped her shoulder.

"Forester," she began, turning.

But the tap turned into a clamp. A vice-like grip holding her in place, forcing her to keep her attention straight ahead.

"Be still," a cold whisper slithered into her ear, "and silent."

The unmistakable pressure of a gun barrel pressed against her temple.

CHAPTER 21

The cold metal of the gun barrel pressed against Artemis' back as she, Cameron, and Jamie were herded through the dark, claustrophobic tunnel system under the school. The dim lighting cast eerie shadows on the damp stone walls. Their footsteps echoed ominously in the confined space, amplifying the sense of dread that weighed heavily on them.

"Keep moving," the harsh voice behind them commanded, punctuating the tense silence.

Artemis clenched her jaw, focusing on the sound of each footstep and the steady rhythm of her breathing. She couldn't afford to let fear cloud her judgment, not when they were all depending on her.

Cameron glanced over at her, his expression grim. Blood trickled down his forehead, and his gun was missing. One wrist was cuffed to the back of the wheelchair in which Jamie Kramer slumped over, still semi-conscious, his eyes still shut.

As they continued deeper into the tunnel, the musty smell of damp earth filled Artemis' nostrils and the echoes of their footsteps haunted the oppressive darkness. Time seemed to stretch out endlessly, the seconds ticking by with agonizing slowness as they marched toward an uncertain fate.

The dim light flickered, casting unsettling shadows around them as they moved forward.

The narrow beam of a flashlight illuminated their path, casting eerie shadows on the damp walls of the tunnel. Each footstep echoed, amplifying the sense of confinement and isolation. Artemis forced herself to focus, analyzing every detail of their surroundings for anything that could offer an advantage.

"Left up ahead," their captor commanded, his voice cold and unforgiving.

As they turned, Artemis caught sight of the figure lurking behind them. The man wore a creepy Halloween mask, the twisted grin and hollow eyes sending chills down her spine. It was like some demented, wart-faced goblin, with bulging, yellow eyes, the sort of mask designed to scare children.

In one hand, he held a camera, recording their every move. Even compared to the rigid threat of the pistol he was pressing into her back, the camera hand looked steady and professional.

Artemis clenched her fists, anger coursing through her veins at the sight. How could they have let this happen? She knew it was a trap and yet when the moment came, they'd all been ambushed just the same.

"Keep moving," the gunman growled when Artemis hesitated for a moment too long.

The dim light from the killer's camera light flickered, casting eerie shadows on the damp walls of the tunnel. The air felt heavy, suffocating. Artemis could hear the sinister hum of delight in his voice as he issued directions to the group.

"Move a little to the right, Agent Forester," the killer commanded softly, his tone dripping with sadistic joy. "I want you in the perfect angle for this shot."

Artemis clenched her fists, anger simmering beneath the surface. She forced herself to take slow, steady breaths, reminding herself that she needed to remain focused and alert if they were going to make it out of this alive.

As they moved deeper into the labyrinth of tunnels, the atmosphere became increasingly oppressive. The air grew hotter and more humid, the echo of their footsteps reverberating throughout the tight space. Artemis knew they were getting close to the boiler room.

"Stop," the killer whispered, the venomous satisfaction in his voice making Artemis' skin crawl. "We're here."

Her heart pounded in her chest as they stepped into the dimly lit boiler room. The walls were lined with rusted pipes and machinery, the stifling heat pressing down on them like a physical weight.

"Agent Forester, against the wall," the killer instructed, the softness of his words only heightening the menace in his voice.

Cameron shot Artemis a weary glance before complying, forced to push Jamie's wheelchair forward until his back pressed against the cold, unforgiving concrete wall. Artemis looked at the two men, her mind racing with potential plans of action. She had to find a way to turn the tables on their captor, and she had to do it soon.

The killer glanced at Cameron once more. He muttered, "Two steps to the right, please. On your mark."

Artemis noticed a white, spray-painted X on the ground.

Cameron growled under his breath but complied with the directive.

The killer took a few hurried steps back toward the metal door, his movements furtive, hesitant, the gun drifting between each of them in turn like a final, silent warning to behave.

He hooked the door behind him with his heel, pulling it open slowly.

The metal door creaked open. He glanced at the figures in the room a final time, before nodding. "Perfect. Just like that." He kept his camera raised, holding it gingerly, as if it were a small bird that might flutter away or be crushed if he held it too loose or too firm. He then stepped through the metal door, back into the hall, hiding himself behind the wall.

Artemis frowned, watching as he fumbled with his gun, slipping it into his waistband. Then, with the same hand, he pulled a second, smaller gun from behind his back. He checked the chamber, nodded once, and shouted, "Only one bullet. So don't try anything funny."

His voice was so strangely normal. In a way, this was more creepy than anything else. He sounded like a banker or a fast-food worker.

He sounded like a person.

Artemis shivered at the realization.

Then, the man in the goblin mask tossed the single-shot gun toward Artemis, the weapon landing with a cold thud at her feet. "Choose," he demanded, his voice distorted by the mask. "One of them dies, or all of you do."

Artemis' eyes flicked between the gun and the two men against the wall, her mind racing. So that was his game, he was playing up a scene, some drama for his audience. But was he really going to just let her have a gun? One bullet or not, Artemis looked down at the weapon suspiciously.

Jamie or Cameron. She knew she couldn't let either of them die—but did the killer know that about her? Did he think the daughter of the convicted Ghost Killer would play along? Perhaps he'd rigged the gun or put a blank in it simply to torture them with the choice?

"Pick it up," the killer urged, amusement lacing his tone.

Reluctantly, Artemis bent down and grabbed the gun, feeling its weight in her hand. She looked at Cameron and Jamie. Jamie was still unconscious, and Cameron had an expression like a shark. No emotion, just determination.

"Time's ticking, my dear," the killer taunted, his own gun and the camera both following the Halloween mask's stare. "I'm not known for my patience."

Artemis lifted the gun, some of the skill she'd picked up guiding her fingers as she checked the safety. For a moment, the barrel strayed away from her friends to the space between them and the killer.

"There's only one bullet, remember!" the madman squawked. He waved his own gun to remind her who had the upper hand.

So it was loaded. *Either that or he's doing an excellent job pretending it is,* Artemis thought. She hesitated, her fingers touching the cold barrel of the gun.

"Enough!" the killer snarled. "Choose now, or I will kill them both!"

Her heart pounded, drowning out every sound except for the blood rushing in her ears. Artemis knew that if she didn't make a decision soon, the killer would carry out his threat.

The killer's wicked grin grew wider behind the large, pronounced mouth hole of his mask as he started the countdown. "Ten... nine... eight..."

Artemis' heart pounded in her chest, a relentless drumbeat echoing in her ears. She closed her eyes, trying to focus on anything but the feeling of cold metal against her sweaty palm. The weight of the gun was unbearable, guilt and fear adding heft to the oiled steel.

"Seven... six... five..."

"Artemis, look at me," Cameron whispered urgently. She opened her eyes, meeting his gaze. In that moment, time seemed to slow down, and she saw something in his eyes—a mix of unflinching resolution and acceptance. It was as if he'd already made the choice for her.

"Four... three..."

"Cam, I can't..." Artemis choked out, tears threatening to fall. Her grip on the gun wavered, and she felt her control slipping away.

"Two..."

"Trust yourself, Artemis," Cameron said softly, never breaking eye contact, never showing fear.

"ONE!"

"NO!" Artemis screamed, her voice raw with emotion. But even as she denied the killer's demands, she knew there was no way out of this hellish predicament. The decision was hers alone to make, and the consequences would be hers to bear.

"Too late!" the killer shouted furiously. "Now, you'll all die together! Unless you do it. RIGHT NOW. Do it! Choose. Do it!"

Artemis' hands trembled as she raised the gun, desperately trying to steady her aim. Her hazel eye shone with unshed tears, while her blue one burned with fury. Cameron's gaze remained locked on hers, unwavering in his faith and acceptance. He swallowed hard, nodding ever so slightly as if to say it was okay.

"Please... forgive me," Artemis whispered, her voice barely audible. With a heavy heart, she squeezed the trigger.

The gunshot reverberated throughout the boiler room, echoing off the grimy walls and rusty pipes. For a brief moment, everything froze—the world suspended in time as the bullet tore through the air.

Cameron crumpled to the ground, the hand cuffed to Jamie's wheelchair jerked the other man forty-five degrees as Forester's muscled body twisted to the floor. His head struck the concrete wall as he slid down, the cuffed arm suspended over him as if trying to pull himself back up by the wheelchair's frame. But his fingers were lifeless, and a moment later, Cameron Forester went still.

"Cam!" Artemis gasped, her face contorted in anguish. The gun slipped from her grasp, clattering onto the cold concrete floor. She wanted to scream, to shout at the top of her lungs, but all that escaped her lips was a choked sob.

She shook her head, unable to find the words to explain her actions. How could she justify choosing one life over another, no matter how necessary it may have seemed? A sick feeling twisted in her stomach, threatening to consume her whole.

"Cam... I'm so sorry," she managed to choke out, silently begging for forgiveness she knew she didn't deserve.

The killer's laughter echoed through the boiler room, a perverse symphony of delight as he reveled in the chaos and despair he had created. Artemis felt her fists clench at the sound, rage simmering just beneath the surface. She struggled to keep her focus on the man behind the Halloween mask, his face distorted by the grinning visage of a demonic goblin.

"Such a beautiful tragedy," the killer cooed, his voice dripping with sadistic glee. "You should be proud, Artemis. I didn't think you had it in you."

"Shut up!" she spat, her eyes blazing with fury. Her heart pounded in her chest, her breaths coming in sharp gasps.

"Of course, now it's two against one," the killer mused, almost casually stepping over Cameron's body. "Do you think you can stop me, Artemis?"

"Enough," Artemis snapped, her mind racing as she searched for any possible way out of this hellish situation. "We played your game. Now let Jamie go! Why are you doing this? What's the point if you just planned on killing us all anyway!"

"Isn't it obvious?" the killer asked, tilting his head slightly as if genuinely curious. "I'm teaching you a lesson. Sometimes, even the smartest people need to learn... fear."

"Is that what this is about?" she demanded, her voice shaking with anger. "You're just some pathetic bully trying to make yourself feel powerful?"

"Pathetic?" the killer replied, his tone suddenly cold. "I wouldn't be so quick to judge, Artemis. After all, you're the one who just shot her boyfriend."

"Shut up!" she screamed, her emotions threatening to boil over. The killer only laughed in response, his sinister cackling filling the air like poison.

She stared at him, at the camera in his hand.

He was aiming it towards them, through the door. His gun was still clutched at a safe distance, away from her.

But the camera?

His darling, darling camera angling for the very best shot? It was so very close.

She was shaking her head, shoulders shuddering, "I... I don't know what I've done," she whispered, her face streaked with fear and anxiety. She tilted her chin, letting the tears flow freely now.

You want a show? I'll give you a show, Artemis thought bitterly. Come get a closeup. You know you want it.

It was a tease. Enough to draw his camera even closer towards her.

He didn't want to miss the perfect shot.

She'd known he wouldn't.

Inwardly, she was cold as steel. No emotion, just focus, like in a blitz match.

But externally, she was a mess. An emotional wreck, designed for his amusement.

And it was working.

He leaned forward, eager, watching her.

"How does it make you feel?" he whispered, jutting the camera greedily in her face. "Hmm?"

She stared into the lens, wiped a fake tear away, and whispered, "It makes me feel like Cameron is wearing a bulletproof vest, you idiot."

And then her emotions changed.

One moment, unhinged, terrified, on the verge of weeping. The next, completely cold. Resolute, eyes narrowed.

He stared at her, blinking, not quite comprehending.

But Cameron let out a faint groan, confirming her words. Though he'd hit his head hard when he'd struck the concrete wall.

"What the hell..." the killer began.

"It's called acting," Artemis whispered.

And then she snatched his camera from his hand.

He'd been protecting his gun. Assuming that's what she would go for.

But no.

No, she couldn't harm him physically with a camera. But she had him pegged now.

She knew who he was dealing with.

And it was going to cost him.

He yelled in horror as she yanked the camera away, and she darted back, clutching her newly claimed prize and desperately hoping she hadn't just condemned them all.

CHAPTER 22

Artemis clutched the camera to her chest, using it as a bullet-proof vest.

Though unlike Cameron's, hers was more of a psychological impediment.

The man in the grotesque mask stared at her, his lips under the flabby, rubber opening, twisted into a snarl.

His gun pointed directly at her head.

But she held the camera up, high overhead now. "These things are fragile," she warned, breathing heavily, her face flushed. "Do you really want to risk it?"

He stared at her, stunned.

It had been the calculated risk. There was nothing this man cared more about than his footage—his gruesome films.

She'd seen it in his posture—in the way his eyes had tracked their movements, an almost greedy expression across his countenance as he attempted to record it all.

And the proof was in the pudding.

She was still alive.

"Lower the gun," she said firmly. She raised the camera in warning as if she were about to smash it.

"Don't!" he yelped.

She allowed herself a small, cold smile.

"Lower the gun," she repeated, more firmly.

His Halloween mask hid his features, but his posture had tensed.

He took a step forward, his gun raised.

"Don't," she warned again.

The man stopped in his tracks, his eyes blazing with rage and frustration. He seemed to be struggling with something deep inside of him, a battle between what he wanted and what he was afraid of losing.

"I will shoot you," he snarled.

"You do that, the camera falls," she replied. "You might even hit it. Imagine that? All that work—destroyed in an instant. I'm not worth that to you, am I? My life isn't anywhere near as valuable to you as this footage."

His trigger finger twitched. She supposed he was imagining wrapping his fingers around her neck, throttling her until she released the grip on his precious recording device.

But she stood her ground, facing a gunman with nothing but a camera for protection.

Suddenly, he turned his weapon, aiming towards where Cameron lay groaning on the ground. Then he swiveled the gun towards Jamie.

"Give it back or I'll kill them both."

Artemis felt her heart flutter. This had been the part she'd feared. The one hitch in the plan.

But she had to stand her ground. She knew that much. If she gave him his camera back, she'd lose all leverage.

And he'd kill them all. There was no doubt at this point.

So she said simply, "No. You hurt them, I smash this."

She raised it again.

"Don't!" he snarled.

"Lower the gun!" she spat.

"I'll kill them. I swear I will!"

"You won't," she retorted, her voice as cold as a winter's breeze.

Artemis knew he was bluffing. The man cared about his camera more than anything. Anyone. His life's work was in her hand.

At least... that was the working theory.

But she held onto it, desperately, clasping to a theory that was her sole hope. She couldn't let her guard down. Not even for a moment.

The man's finger twitched on the trigger once more. Artemis braced herself for the worst.

But she didn't back down.

Sometimes, when faced with fear, a soul had a choice. It was a difficult choice, but a very simple one. To concede or not. To give in, or not.

And in that moment she'd damned all the possibilities in her mind.

She didn't care.

She'd chosen a path, and she was sticking to it.

Cameron was now sitting up, and she could see him out of the corner of her eye.

Jamie Kramer had roused as well but looked confused and scared. His eyes were blinking rapidly, and he was breathing in quick puffs.

Forester was calm, watchful, like a wolf waiting for the opportune moment to strike.

This had always been the difference between the two men. Cameron with teeth—predatory in some ways. But a fearsome protector. Jamie, on the other hand, was innocent and safe. But also desperate to keep some semblance of normalcy.

And in that moment, her heart made a choice that her head hadn't quite comprehended.

Nothing was normal about her life.

And in a way... she wasn't sure it was ever meant to be.

Artemis felt her hands shaking as she continued to hold the camera up. She could hear the man breathing heavily, his finger still on the trigger.

And then...

Finally...

He gritted his teeth and lowered the gun. His arm trembled, but he didn't raise it again.

Artemis kept her gaze steady on him as she slowly lowered the camera back to her chest. She could feel her heart pounding in her chest like a frantic drumbeat as adrenaline coursed through her veins.

Neither of them spoke for what felt like an eternity—a tense stand-off. A stalemate that could only be broken by one of them making a move. But neither seemed willing to budge in their position; both too stubborn or too scared to make the first move.

The silence was deafening as they stared each other down, neither one willing to give an inch—until finally, Artemis said, "Lower the gun."

She took a step towards him.

"Put it on the ground," she said, a bit more loudly.

She took another step.

He tensed. His eyes flashed.

"There are more cameras," he snapped. And in a way, it felt as if he were attempting to convince himself.

She could see the change in his eyes—a decision being reached.

His gun arm raised, but she surged into him, closing the distance with one step.

A gunshot resounded in her ears.

Her shoulder had caught his forearm at the same time, sending the gun wide.

She sent him clattering to the ground, under her weight.

Had the bullet hit someone?

No time to look.

She fought for control of the gun with the masked man.

He was larger than her, stronger than her.

She could feel her breath coming rapidly and could feel her stomach twisting like a coiled serpent.

She struggled with her fingers clasping at his wrist, trying to hold him down.

She heard Cameron grunting behind her, willing his beaten and bruised form to rise from the ground based on sheer willpower alone.

But he was still disoriented. He'd struck his head, and the gunshot to his vest had been like a sledgehammer.

The man in the mask was snarling fiercely, trying to strangle her now.

First, she was on top, then he was.

The two of them rolled out into the dark tunnel, and Artemis felt her shoulder brush against the dusty, red brick of the wall.

The gun was still between them, and she could feel the strength of his grip on it.

He was trying to get leverage, but her legs were wrapped around his waist.

The two of them wrestled for control of the weapon, their bodies locked together in a desperate, back-and-forth fight. They were both dripping with sweat now, their faces inches apart as they fought for control.

Finally, Artemis managed to break away from him and scrambled backward towards the entrance to the hallway. But he lunged forward again in an instant, grabbing her arm and pulling her back into the darkness. She felt herself being dragged backward until her back slammed against the cold brick wall. He was on top of her now—his eyes wild with rage as he held her down with one hand while reaching for the gun with another.

She fought to keep her grip on the gun as they rolled, each trying to gain the upper hand. Her heart was pounding in her chest, and her breath came in short gasps as she struggled against him.

Finally, she managed to twist the gun out of his grip.

But he had allowed this.

Last minute, she spotted the knife.

She watched, as if in slow motion, as the blade scythed towards her.

He was staring at her neck.

She reacted almost on instinct—reaching up with one hand, snatching at his mask, and tugging it an inch down.

At the same time, she bucked her hips and twisted her neck away from the blade.

The weapon clattered harmlessly off the ground, but now, the man couldn't see.

His mask was obscuring his vision.

The taunting, grotesque plastic covering intended to elicit fear now only left him looking silly—blinded by his own performative garb.

Artemis tumbled back, gun in hand. She rose to her feet, her voice trembling.

"Stay down," she gasped, her voice hoarse.

The man sneered at her, but he didn't move, his fingers scrabbling to adjust the mask.

For a moment, he just lay there, gasping for breath. Then, Artemis heard a groan from behind her. She turned her head to see Cameron struggling to his feet, a hand pressed against his side where the bullet had hit his vest.

"Cameron, are you okay?" she asked, still keeping one eye on the man beneath her.

"I'm fine," he grunted. "Just a bruise." The former cage fighter gave the cuffs linking him to Jamie's chair a couple quick, rattling tugs, then he dragged the other man, chair and all, closer to

Artemis and the pinned killer. "Hey," he gave the masked man a swift kick in the ribs. "Keys?"

Despite the killer's obstinate silence, Cameron soon found the cuff key in a pocket, but not before Artemis made out the whisper of a growled threat from her scarred boyfriend. "I know it doesn't feel like it. But this is you being *lucky,*" he told the killer. "If she were the one cuffed to this chair, and I had the gun, the last air you ever breathed would have been through that cheap, dime-store mask."

When Forester turned back to her, he was all grin, jangling the little cuff key and waggling his eyebrows.

Artemis nodded, letting out a sigh of relief that Cameron didn't seem to be any worse for wear. Then she turned her attention back to the man on the ground.

"Who are you?" she demanded, pressing the gun against his temple.

He didn't answer, just glared up at her with cold, calculating eyes.

"Answer me," she hissed.

Still, he said nothing.

She stared into the mask. She didn't recognize those eyes. Didn't know this man.

She realized how often one's curiosity could attempt to unmask men like this. To try and see what lurked underneath.

How often had she seen it on the news?

Shootings, murders, muggings, attacks... It all ended in the revelation of the mugshot. Or the whodunit.

But standing there, in that moment, she realized she really, truly—as deep as her bones—didn't care.

She didn't care who he was.

What he looked like.

Why he did what he did, or why he wanted what he wanted.

"You're just like the rest of them," she murmured softly.

And then, with trembling hands, she reached back, accepting the handcuffs from Cameron.

"Get on your stomach," she commanded. "Turn over."

He did, still glaring at her from behind his paltry, thin, pathetic mask.

She let out a final, long breath. She glanced at Jamie and met his gaze.

Confusion remained in his eyes as he watched her cuff the killer.

"Are you alright?" she said, her tone gentle.

Jamie stared at her, his eyes full of tears. He then bent his head, and released a slow breath, staring at his knees.

As if he couldn't quite bear looking at her.

Or perhaps he was simply tired.

She didn't know.

But Cameron stood at her side.

There hadn't been any doubt.

But if there had been, her heart and her mind were now in agreement.

Under her breath, she murmured, "Were you serious about moving?"

"Hmm?" Cameron said. He was hauling the killer to his feet.

"Were you serious? About all of us moving."

"Yeah," he said simply with a shrug. He looked a bit confused as if he couldn't understand why she might ask such a thing.

He reached for the killer's mask, but Artemis caught his hand.

"Keep it on him."

CHAPTER 23

Sirens wailed, and Artemis leaned exhausted against the hood of their car, watching as the killer—still in his mask, at her request—was sped away in the back of a police cruiser.

Jamie was gone too, now. Just like that—as if fingers had snapped, and everything had changed.

Jamie was no longer part of her life.

But he was alive, and she was glad for that.

To keep him safe, though, for his sake—she had to keep moving.

Cameron sat on the hood of the car next to her. The two of them both stared at the red brick, gothic school the killer had chosen as his climactic setting.

Artemis' eyes moved towards where a couple of cops were holding a whispered conference, wide-eyed and fearful.

Likely discussing the officer whose wife had been kidnapped.

A bluff.

It had turned out to be a lie.

The killer had done the same with Jessica Parker. Using a red dot light to pretend it was a rifle scope.

Lies within lies—all packaged in fear and terror.

Artemis frowned, shivering as she considered it all. She let out a long sigh, leaning her head against Forester's shoulder and staring out from her perch on the hood of the car.

The dancing lights of the police cars were like a private fireworks show.

"I think we should," she said abruptly, rushing the words out before she could change her mind.

"Hmm?"

"I think we should move. All of us."

Cameron tensed. He glanced at her. "Really?"

"Yeah. Really."

"To Turkey?"

"Why not?"

"No reason..." He grinned. "I've been doing some reading, actually."

"You can read?"

"I like the pictures, but sometimes the letters give me funny feelings in my brain."

"It's nice to know you're a man of letters, Forester."

He smirked. "Not all of us can be Backgammon savants."

"Mhmm. I play backgammon about as well as you kiss."

He shook his head. "Too many words for me. Didn't get it. I'll take it as a compliment."

"It was an insult."

"Nah. Too late. Compliment taken. Anywhoo—I've been doing some reading. Did you know the beaches in Turkey are some of the most beautiful in the world? Crystal clear water, white sands, and plenty of sunshine." Cameron's eyes sparkled with excitement. "We could leave all this behind and start fresh. Just you and me."

"And Helen, and my dad," she said, frowning and glancing at him.

"Yeah! Yeah, that's what I meant."

"Was it?" she pressed.

He hesitated, sighed.

"Don't lie to me, Cameron."

He looked at her. "For you, yes. Truly. They're welcome because they matter to you." He shrugged. "Eventually, I'm sure they'll matter to me too, Checkers."

"I hope so."

He winked. "If not, so what. You'll be there. Good enough for me."

Artemis smiled at the thought, a warmth spreading through her. She listened to Cameron prattle a bit more about the different types of unique foods in Turkey. Something called *Cop sis* most fascinated him. It roughly translated to trash meat. To Artemis, the mention of an *Adana Kebap* was more interesting.

Could they really do it?

Uproot everything—take everyone and move to another country?

A fresh start.

Not just for her, but for Helen, for her father... for Cameron?

She could feel the warmth building in her chest, and she allowed herself a faint flicker of a smile.

CHAPTER 24

The sun dipped low in the sky, casting long shadows across the opulent study. In an armchair that seemed to swallow him whole, a wealthy man known only as 'the soldier' lounged, his prosthetic arm glinting in the fading light. He idly tapped its metallic fingers on the rich mahogany of the side table, creating a rhythmic clink that filled the room. The butler, a short and furtive man named Reginald, stood at attention nearby, waiting for his master's command.

"Reginald," the soldier drawled, not bothering to look up from the newspaper he held in his other hand. His voice was thick and authoritative, every syllable laden with power. "Fetch me another glass of brandy."

"Of course, sir," Reginald replied, his voice barely above a whisper as he scurried toward the drink cabinet. The soldier watched him through half-lidded eyes, a subtle smirk playing on his lips. There was something about Reginald's subservient demeanor that amused him—perhaps it was the way the butler seemed to shrink under his gaze, or how he was always so eager to please.

"Be quick about it," the soldier said, his tone sharp as a knife's edge. "I have matters to attend to." His mind wandered to the two individuals who had recently piqued his interest. He needed to know more about them, and Reginald would be instrumental in gathering the necessary information. After all, loyalty was a trait the soldier valued most in his servants.

"Right away, sir," Reginald stammered, returning with the brandy and carefully filling the soldier's glass. The liquid shimmered like amber beneath the dim light, and the soldier took a slow, deliberate sip, savoring the warmth as it spread through him. His gaze lingered on the butler, who seemed to be holding his breath.

"Is there something else on your mind?" the soldier asked, his voice deceptively gentle. He had a unique talent for sensing unease in others, and he enjoyed exploiting it.

"Nothing, sir," Reginald replied hastily, visibly swallowing. "I just—"

"Good," the soldier cut him off, returning his attention to the newspaper. "Do you think I'm crippled?" he said softly.

The butler tensed, sensing the trap question. He swallowed, staring at his master.

The soldier's prosthetic arm glistened under the chandelier's light as he flexed his fingers, each digit moving with a mechanical precision that belied its human appearance. This advanced piece of engineering had been custom-made for him, replacing the limb he had lost during a time he rarely spoke of. It served not only as a reminder of his victories but also as an emblem of his quest for vengeance.

"Any news on Cameron Forester?" the soldier asked, changing the topic before his butler could answer the initial question.

Reginald pulled something from his pocket, now clutching a small leather-bound notebook. "Yes, sir. I've managed to track their movements," he said, his voice trembling slightly under the soldier's intense gaze. "I have someone keeping an eye on them as we speak."

"Good. Make sure they're not alerted to our presence," the soldier ordered, shifting the weight of his prosthetic arm, testing its capabilities by picking up a crystal glass from the table. Not even a hint of a tremor betrayed the artificial nature of the limb. He raised it to his lips and took a sip of the aged whiskey within, savoring the burn as it slid down his throat.

"Of course, sir," Reginald replied. He scribbled something in his notebook before looking back at the soldier. "They seem to be growing more confident, perhaps even reckless."

"Reckless, you say?" The soldier arched an eyebrow, his interest piqued. He pondered the implications for a moment, his thoughts clouded by the thrill of the hunt. "That could work in our favor. Keep a close watch on them. Report any changes immediately."

"Absolutely, sir."

"Tell me. What do you think is the most fitting location for Artemis and Cameron to experience the consequences of their actions?"

Reginald shifted uneasily, his fidgeting betraying the calm demeanor he'd cultivated over years of service. "Well, sir," he hesitated, his thoughts racing as he considered the possible outcomes. "I believe their vulnerability lies in their complacency. They've grown too comfortable in their surroundings."

"Go on." The soldier leaned forward, his interest sharpening like the edge of a blade.

"Artemis' apartment seems to be their primary meeting place," Reginald continued, recalling the patterns he'd observed during his diligent surveillance. "It's where they let their guard down, where they believe they're safe from prying eyes."

"Interesting." The soldier's mind churned with possibilities, each thought darker than the last. He could picture the terror in their eyes when they realized that the hunter had become the hunted.

"Prepare a plan, Reginald," he ordered. "I want every detail accounted for. This will be a lesson they won't forget. Leave nothing to chance. I want them to know who's responsible for their suffering,"

And then, in a flourish, the soldier rose from his seat, the intricate metalwork of his arm casting a web of shadows on the polished wooden floor. His fingers flexed, each metallic digit moving with a smooth, unnerving grace. The sound of gears and hydraulics whispered through the room, a symphony of mechanical precision.

The soldier's attention was drawn to the gun rack at the back of the room, its polished wood frame encasing an array of firearms that gleamed menacingly in the dim light. Each weapon had been meticulously cared for, their barrels and triggers free from even a speck of dust, reflecting the soldier's dedication to his craft.

"Let's see what we have here..." he murmured, moving closer to inspect the assortment.

"Ah, the Remington 870," he mused, running his fingers over the cool metal of the shotgun's barrel. "Powerful, but not quite suitable for our purposes tonight."

His icy eyes scanned the collection, evaluating each firearm based on its attributes and their intended use for the evening. He paused at a sleek, black Glock 19, its compact design perfect for concealment and close-quarters combat.

"Too easy," he muttered under his breath, dismissing it with a shake of his head. The soldier was seeking a challenge, something that would truly test his skills.

As he continued to peruse the weapons, his eyes flicked sharply, a predatory glint that matched his growing anticipation. Finally, his gaze settled on the perfect choice: an intricately engraved Winchester Model 70 bolt-action rifle, its long-range capabilities ideal for picking off targets with precision.

He cradled the rifle in his remaining arm as if it were a precious treasure. As he admired its craftsmanship, the soldier couldn't help but feel a sense of exhilaration. It was a feeling that reminded him of why he had chosen this path in the first place—the thrill of the hunt, the power over life and death.

But beneath that excitement, there was also a nagging doubt, one that whispered seductive half-truths and unsettling questions. He knew that his butler had reservations about their plans, and the soldier couldn't help but wonder if Reginald's loyalty would waver when the time came to act.

"Reginald," he said softly.

"Y-yes, sir?"

"Which would you recommend?"

"Sorry?"

"Which weapon?"

"Me, sir?"

"Yes. You."

"Sir, might I suggest the FN SCAR 17S?" Reginald offered hesitantly, knowing full well the soldier preferred to make his own decisions. "It has excellent accuracy at both close and long range, and its adaptability would serve you well against both of, er, them."

"An excellent suggestion, Reginald" the soldier agreed, his eyes fixated on the sleek, black semi-automatic rifle.

A satisfied nod accompanied his decision as he turned to face Reginald.

"Prepare the car, Reginald," he commanded, the second rifle held firmly in his grip. "It's time we paid Agent Forester a visit..."

"Understood, sir" Reginald replied, bowing slightly and making his way towards the door, leaving the soldier alone with his thoughts.

The soldier's gaze lingered on the chosen weapon, his fingers tracing the cold steel and smooth edges of the 17S rifle. The air around him seemed to hum with anticipation, as if the room itself understood the gravity of the situation. He slowly exhaled, feeling the weight of his decision settle onto his shoulders.

As he waited for Reginald to return, the soldier's thoughts wandered to Cameron.

The man who'd tried to kill him.

The man who thought he was dead.

He smiled now.

Cameron had wanted vengeance for his wife's death. And now ... he'd resurrected her. Artemis Blythe... The spitting image of Cameron's deceased beloved.

But the soldier hadn't been killed in that explosion. He'd suffered—he'd lost an arm. But Cameron would suffer too, now.

The soldier nodded resolutely.

He imagined the shock that would register on Cameron's face when he realized, the fear that would grip his heart as he understood. An involuntary smile tugged at the corner of his mouth; it was a scenario he found deeply satisfying.

But even as his mind reveled in these dark fantasies, the soldier knew that he could not afford to underestimate his prey. They had proven themselves to be formidable opponents, and he would need every ounce of his skill and cunning to bring them to heel.

"Focus," he muttered under his breath, silencing the whirlwind of thoughts that threatened to consume him. "This is no time for distractions."

The sound of an engine purring to life outside snapped him back to reality. The car was ready, and it was time to set his plan into motion. Gripping the rifle tightly, he flung his second over his shoulder on a leather strap, and then he strode towards the door, a slight, excited skip to his step.

Hunting was supposed to be fun, after all.

What's Next for Artemis?

Blood flows quicker than water...

From the palatial halls of the Blue Mosque to the arching turrets of the Bosphorus Bridges, death stalks our heroine even to beautiful foreign shores.

A fresh start brings Artemis to Istanbul, but the death of a local chess prodigy on a ferry boat under the most famous bridge in the city threatens to compromise everything.

Authorities suspect an honor killing, but Artemis believes the truth is something far more sinister. Her investigation brings her to the doors of a local police station in a small, Turkish town, headed by an ambitious police chief whose town is caught in a family blood feud that threatens to consume everyone and everything it touches.

For the first time in her life, Artemis believes her family might start afresh, but will this new scrutiny bring everything crashing down? Or will she be able to endear herself to the locals by solving this grisly murder?

ALSO BY GEORGIA WAGNER

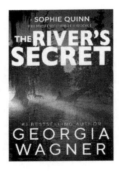

A cold knife, a brutal laugh.

Then the odds-defying escape.

Once a hypnotist with her own TV show, now, Sophie Quinn works as a full-time consultant for the FBI. Everything changed six years ago. She can still remember that horrible night. Slated to be the River Killer's tenth victim, she managed to slip her bindings and barely escape where so many others failed. Her sister wasn't so lucky.

And now the killer is back.

Two PHDs later, she's now a rising star at the FBI. Her photographic memory helps solve crimes, but also helps her to never forget. She saw the River Killer's tattoo. She knows what he sounds like. And now, ten years later, he's active again.

Sophie Quinn heads back home to the swamps of Louisiana, along the Mississippi River, intent on evening the score and finding the man who killed her sister. It's been six years since she's been home, though. Broken relationships and shattered dreams exist among the bayous, the rivers, the waterways and swamps of Louisiana; can Sophie find her way home again? Or will she be the River Killer's next victim to float downstream?

ALSO BY GEORGIA WAGNER

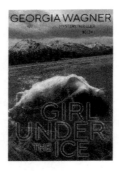

**Once a rising star in the FBI, with the best case closure
rate of any investigator, Ella Porter is now exiled to a small
gold mining town bordering the wilderness of Alaska.
The reason for her new assignment? She allowed a prolific
serial killer to escape custody.**

But what no one knows is that she did it on purpose.

The day she shows up in Nome, bags still unpacked, the wife of the richest gold miner in town goes missing. This is the second woman to vanish in as many days. And it's up to Ella to find out what happened.

Assigning Ella to Nome is no accident, either. Though she swore she'd never return, Ella grew up in the small, gold mining town, treated like royalty as a child due to her own family's wealth. But like all gold tycoons, the Porter family secrets are as dark as Ella's own.

Want to know more?

Greenfield press is the brainchild of bestselling author Steve Higgs. He specializes in writing fast paced adventurous mystery and urban fantasy with a humorous lilt. Having made his money publishing his own work, Steve went looking for a few 'special' authors whose work he believed in.

Georgia Wagner was the first of those, but to find out more and to be the first to hear about new releases and what is coming next, you can join the Facebook group by copying the following link into your browser – www.facebook.com/GreenfieldPress.

ABOUT THE AUTHOR

Georgia Wagner worked as a ghost writer for many, many years before finally taking the plunge into self-publishing. Location and character are two big factors for Georgia, and getting those right allows the story to flow seamlessly onto the page. And flow it does, because Georgia is so prolific a new term is required to describe the rate at which nerve-tingling stories find their way into print.

When not found attached to a laptop, Georgia likes spending time in local arboretums, among the trees and ponds. An avid cultivator of orchids, begonias, and all things floral, Georgia also has a strong penchant for art, paintings, and sculptures. A many-decades long passion for mystery novels and years of chess tournament experience makes Georgia the perfect person to pen the Artemis Blythe series.

Printed in Great Britain
by Amazon